When not being an acclaimed fantasy writer, Jo M. Thomas enjoys historical fencing. Her previous novels include 25 Ways to Kill A Werewolf, A Pack of Lies and Fool If You Think It's Over.

Other Side Book contributions by Jo M. Thomas

The Knights Daughter
Sea Terrors
The Second Christmas Book of Ghosts

ISLE OF RAVENS

BY JO M. THOMAS

Other Side Books

This edition published in 2021 by
Other Side Books
Glasgow G51 3SJ

www.othersidebooks.co.uk

Copyright © Jo M. Thomas 2021

Cover illustration © Mark Hetherington 2021

ISBN: 9798490951919

All rights reserved.
No part of this publication may be reproduced,
stored or transmitted in any form without the express
written permission of the publisher.

The moral right of Jo M. Thomas to be identified
as the author of this work has been asserted by him in
accordance with the Copyright, Designs and Patents
Act 1988.

The moral right of Mark Hetherington to be identified
as the artists of this work has been asserted to them in
accordance with the Coypright, Designs and Patents
Act 1988.

This is tale is an attempt to describe events that really did not happen by people who were not there. There may still be some truth left in it.

Jo M. Thomas

10th April, 2019

Contents

Chapter One: In which the true King returns .12

Chapter Two: In which a loyal knight is rewarded 21

The Tale of Blondel as told by the Countess .31

Chapter Three: In which the Countess is offended 43

Chapter Four: In which the Earl begs leave ..52

Chapter Five: In which the Earl returns 62

The Tale of Bisclavret as told by the Earl ..70

Chapter Six: In which a marriage is made 84

Chapter Seven: In which the Earl runs away a second time 93

Chapter Eight: In which words are exchanged 102

The Tale of The Loathly Lady as told by the Earl 112

Chapter Nine: In which a great storm breaks 127

Chapter Ten: In which no bridges are built .137

Chapter Eleven: In which a port is rebuilt .146

The Tale of Graelent, as told by the Countess 155

Chapter Twelve: In which a heart is broken .170

Chapter Thirteen: In which ravens fly 179

Chapter Fourteen: In which the King returns 189

The Tale of Ys, as told by the Mistress 198

Chapter Fifteen: In which the Mistress is rewarded 211

Chapter Sixteen: In which friends are reunited 220

The Tale of L'Île des Corbeaux, as told by Jo M. Thomas 228

Chapter One: In which the true King returns

There was once a great city at the mouth of the great Abus[1], on a large sand bar where the river is sluggish and thick with black silt and meets the iron-grey of the North Sea[2]. This city was the Isle of Ravens[3] and, despite the wooden frames of the buildings, it was said to be a second Camelot and the true capital of the North.

The grand stone docks and quays had been built at great expense with the stone carefully imported from upstream. They sheltered a fleet unmatched outside of London and more than a thousand hearths were taxed within the city's walls. There were even green fields, although narrow and muddy, within the ditches and embankments that enclosed the island and its causeway.

---

1 The Abus is another name for the Humber that has long since fallen out of use.
2 Currently, there is a narrow sand spit: Spurn, Spurn Head or Spurn Spit.
3 There was an Old Ravenser, a Ravenser Odd and a Ravenspurn that have all been lost to the North Sea in the Middle Ages. None of them match this description.

It was the beating, working heart of a great fiefdom, built to be the gateway to England by an earl4 who intended to be the gatekeeper and charge accordingly. It was so well loved by this earl and his family that they made it their home away from the Royal court. Indeed, the first building raised was said to be their great palace, another expensive import of stone facing the second building in the settlement -- a small wattle and daub chapel dedicated to St Mary the Virgin, Lady of the Sea.

The port grew such that the king of the time gave the earl an unkindness5, bred from the royal ravens of the White Tower6, to signify the port's importance.7 And it was here that the very same king's son landed when he returned from exile to

---

4   Ravenser Odd was apparently founded by a William de Forz -- either the 3rd Earl of Aumale (Albemarle) and Lord of Holderness or his son, the 4th Earl -- around 1240.
5   A flock of ravens.
6   The White Tower is the original keep of the Tower of London, first built (in stone) in the 1080s by William Conqueror. It was a royal residence right up the 16th Century.
7   This appears to be an attempt to explain the name of the port. However, although ravens would have been quite a common bird in the actual time-frame, the alleged location isn't an area known for the large trees that ravens like.

reclaim his throne from his usurping half-brother.8 He came when the Isle of Ravens was in the hands of the founding earl's daughter, the Countess.9

The true King's ships docked on an evening tide, simple merchant vessels that hung low with some heavy cargo and wouldn't raise an eyebrow. He did not escape speculation, though, as the ships' captains were all Dutchman quite well-known to the locals for their hard-working mentality -- yet they and their crews went straight to the city's inns.

A couple of children, too young to be drafted into work and too poor to be at school, wandered close enough to hear the jingle of metal and spread the news. The few adults who heard were wise enough to identify the sound as horse harnesses. The city guard ignored them.10

---

8 Henry IV landed at Ravenspurn in 1399 on his way to dethroning his cousin, Richard II, and Edward IV landed by the same town in 1471, returning from exile to dethrone his relative, Henry VI. Neither match up with this King.
9 The most likely model is Hawise, 2nd Countess of Aumale, who died in 1214. However, Ravenser Odd, the most similar setting, was founded by her son or grandson.
10 This suggests the Countess was expecting such a mysterious cargo.

It was well after nightfall when all but the guards were in bed that someone crept from one of the ships -- followed by another, and another, and another, and another, until there were five men indistinguishable from the city guards standing on the quay. The guards they resembled turned a blind eye if they noticed at all.

The five men walked to the palace where the guards did notice them, crossing polearms against their entry through the closed gate.

"We are here to see the earl11," said one, removing his helmet. "Announce us."

Another, who was the King incognito, whispered in the spokesman's ear.

"He is expecting us," said the spokesman and he pointed to a lighted candle in an arrow slit.

The two guards at the gate conferred.

"The earl is dead," one guard finally said to the five men. "He died last month. Everyone knows that."

"Well, someone is expecting us," said the spokesman and he pointed once again to the lighted candle.

---

11 They will mean the Countess's husband.

The guard shrugged. "They could be expecting anyone. It could be a kitchen maid signalling her fisherman. Not that he would get in, either."

"We're not here for a kitchen maid," said the spokesman.

The guards conferred again before one of them knocked on the closed gate. "We have men here who claim to be here on the earl's business."

There was a muffled "Who?"

The guards looked expectantly at the five men.

"Friends," was all the spokesman said and the others remained silent.

"There's five of them," said a guard. "Dressed like soldiers."

Unseen footsteps hurried away and, after some uncomfortable moments of time, returned.

"Let them in," someone gasped on the other side of the gates. Even as the words were spoken, the bolts inside were being drawn with loud and heavy metallic groans. "Her Ladyship is expecting them."

The guards uncrossed their polearms as the gate-leaves swung open. Somewhat unnecessarily, one of them said, "You may enter."

The five men walked forward and the gatekeeper who had waited behind the gate, now breathless from his exertions, motioned they should follow him. The gatekeeper led them to the palace's great hall, where the countess sat alone in fine black velvets on a throne that rivalled the grandness of the King's own.

Four out of the five men bowed as they were presented but the King incognito did not. She acknowledged them with a nod and a smile before standing and walking towards them. When she was in easy speaking rather than shouting distance of the King, she dropped into a deep curtsey.

"Your Majesty."

The gatekeeper gasped and hurriedly dropped into a bow of his own.

The King, no longer incognito, removed his helmet so that his dark face was revealed instead of hidden by the shadows. He gave the countess permission to stand in his presence.

"I am afraid you have missed my late husband by a matter of weeks," she said. "Thankfully, his men saw fit to confess my late husband's plans so that I could fulfil his duties."

The King said nothing.

His spokesman, however, asked, "You have the men and arms prepared?"

"My affinity[12] awaits you upstream, Your Majesty," the Countess said. "I will send a pilot with you to take your ships to the meeting place."

"I thank you for your loyalty, lady," said the King.

"And you have not forewarned the Usurper?" asked the spokesman.

The Countess glared at him. "Just because my first husband was a supporter of the Usurper does not mean I am!"[13]

"As you say, my lady," the spokesman replied but he did not sound convinced.

The countess spat, "He died, and you married

---

12 In this case, she will mean the lesser nobles, knights and men-at-arms intended to fulfil her (or her late husband's) military commitments.
13 The real Hawise's husbands were all loyal to the kings of their time (Henry II, Richard I and then John). The later two husbands were chosen for her by Richard I and it's likely the the first was a king's choice as well.

me to one of your own supporters before the Usurper took the throne. How could I have any hand in the Usurper's tricks? How could he trust me as the wife of your supporter?"

"Indeed, my lady, I wonder how he -- as clever as my younger brother is -- could let you keep your fine situation," said the King.

The Countess curtseyed again. "Forgive me for my outburst, Your Majesty."

The King smiled. "You have done nothing wrong in this matter. However, it now occurs to me that, to ensure your loyalty continues, I had better give you another Earl."

The Countess was stunned enough to step back. She opened her mouth to speak but nothing came out.

"My companion here is fine and loyal," the King continued, pointing at the spokesman. "I have promised him a great heiress' hand as a reward for his service to me, as my companion in captivity14. Perhaps you are that heiress or can be."

"But, Your Majesty," said the spokesman.

"My husband has only just died, Your Majesty,

---

14 The real Hawise's third marriage, to Baldwin de Béthune, did happen because of such promises.

it would be unseemly to--"

"We will stay long enough to see you wed," said the King. "Then we will leave you and the bright new Earl to enjoy your honeymoon as you wish, while I reclaim my throne from my brother."

The spokesman's face wrinkled with distaste. "As you command, Your Majesty."

"My dearest friend, this is not an insult," the King said softly, "Who else can I trust with such a mission?"

Chapter Two: In which a loyal knight is rewarded

The King refused to wait for the Countess's wedding.

"Send a servant to rouse a chapel priest," he insisted.

The Countess was slow than he liked to call a servant and the King's patience frayed as they waited for someone to attend. When one of her two lady's maids arrived, it was the King who barked out instructions.

"The Countess has a desire to be wed," said the King. "Fetch a priest and meet us in the chapel."

The Countess herself was politely escorted by the King and his four companions through her palace gates and to the little wattle and daub building.

"The late earl promised, when he married you, to enlarge God's house on this island," the King commented.

"It serves the local population well enough," said the Countess. "The seats are rarely full."

And the King and his companions frowned.

Another voice said, a chaplain15 hurrying

beside the Countess's serving woman, "At least, with the late Earl's donations, the chapel is now a chantry."

"I'm sure the Abbot16 was grateful for it," said the King, "if only because of the extra funds, but should he not have used some of the coin to improve, to impose God's presence here--or even just his abbey's own power--in a great port such as this Ravens' Isle?"

It was the Chaplain's turn to frown.

"I don't think it's a matter for the middle of the night," the King's companion, the soon-to-be Earl said. "But I am sure the Countess and I will discuss it."

The King laughed, cheered rather than angered by the correction. "Of course. You are right, as

---

15 In this instance, it simply means a priest (possibly the only priest) attached a chapel.
16 Ravenserodd was within Easington Parish, part of the York Diocese. However, the founding Earl was a descendent of the Earl of Aumale (Albemarle) who founded Meaux Abbey near Beverley in 1151. The story appears to assume that they would send for religious guidance from the monastery rather than the cathedral.

ever, my friend."

But the companion's own face remained sour and frowning.

The Countess gave her own small, bitter laugh and took the Chaplain's arm. "Perhaps we should await my groom away from the coldness of the night."

The Chaplain looked a little confused but accepted the direction. Any protestations about the Countess marrying too soon were swallowed by the wooden shell of the Chapel of St Mary when the door closed behind them.

"I promised you the hand of a heiress," said the King. "The Countess here owns all of this county and almost as large a share of France.17 Are you not pleased with your match, my dear friend?"

The companion shook his head. "I never desired the hand of an heiress. I wish only to serve you as best I can, with my sword in hand as I defend you."

The other three companions coughed and shuffled in their embarrassment.

"This is how you can best serve me right

---

17 An exaggeration--but not by much if she is modelled on Hawise.

now," the King said softly. "You can hold the greatest gateway into England against traitors and enemies, just as her late husband did before you."

The companion bowed his head. The King had swept into the chapel before the words "As Your Majesty wishes," were forced out.

The companion's words of acceptance were no less forced during the underplayed ceremony and the Countess also showed no signs of eagerness. The Chaplain only grew more confused about the unhappy couple's reasons for marriage. He had not been introduced to the King and had no reason to suppose that the armed man, although obviously the commander of the other four, had any power to insist on the wedding. He could only assume that it was the Countess's wish, no matter the impropriety of marrying so soon after being widowed.

Uneasy, the Chaplain finished the ritual as quickly as he could and then offered, "My sincerest congratulations to the happy couple," before hurrying back to his bed.

The King was scarcely any slower, clapping the new Earl on the shoulder with a hearty "Congratulations! Bed your new wife well!" before striding out of the chapel, his remaining companions flanking him.

The new Earl stood frozen at the altar.

"You look like you're about to cry," said the Countess.

The Earl replied, "Possibly. I have helped His Majesty plan this campaign for years. It is frustrating to watch him leave and trust that others will be able to play their parts without my prompting."

"They will perform perfectly adequately without you," said the Countess.

"I have no doubt of that," said the Earl. "But that only hurts all the more."

The Countess snarled, "I have been given a whipped puppy instead of a man."

The Earl smiled at her. "I thought I had been given you, not the other way around."

When she would have stormed from the small wooden chapel, he found room to reach the door before her and hold it open.

"My lady," he said and bowed.

The Countess swept through the rustic doorway.

"May I walk you to your chambers?" he asked.

He didn't take her arm straight away and it was enough to make the Countess stop to look at him.

"May I?" he asked.

She held out her hand and he rested it on the back of his own.

"Thank you," the Earl said.

And the Countess found herself replying, "You are welcome, my lord."

He led her gently across the street to the palace gatehouse, where guards leapt to attention and opened wooden gates without being prompted. They should, perhaps, have been guarding the chapel, too, but the Countess had not commanded them to follow and it had not been the Earl's place to do so before the wedding.

"You treat me like a fine horse," said the Countess.

The Earl smiled again but did not answer.

"I am not a pet or your property," she said. "I am the Countess of this land, the true Lord of this city despite my sex."

The Earl said, "I am a knight and a champion of the field.18 I know nothing of running estates and managing ports."

"Are you asking me to teach you how to be an Earl?" asked the Countess. "Or simply expecting me to continue in my work so that you can accept the praise?"

"If it is your work, I am hardly likely to be praised for it," the Earl replied.

The Countess's face soured even further as if she was about to hawk and spit at her new husband. He even drew back a fraction and her fingertips, which had barely brushed the back of his gauntlet as they walked together, lost contact altogether.

"My lady," he said. It was half plea and half reminder of her status.

She forced a smile but there was no sweetness, faux or otherwise. "My late husband was not so generous."

"I did not know him," said the Earl. "I don't know what kind of man he was, other than loyal to the King."

"And that is the most important thing," the

---

18 The Earl probably means that he takes part in jousting or other competitions -- and presumably war to have been planning this campaign.

Countess said.

"For the King, anyway," said the Earl, "and it is the King who chose the match."

The Countess sniffed. "I would rather that the King chose a good Earl than a good servant."

"There are many nobles among the King's servants," the Earl said, as if it were the same thing.

"They are not necessarily good at running their estates," said the Countess in a level voice. "They spend too much time following their King to know anything of running estates. The better ones simply have servants of their own to do that for them."19

"Our King. Then I can only apologise for being a simple knight with no land or servants of my own," said the Count.

The Countess's smile was no longer forced but was more bitter than vinegar. "I have no doubt that you are a good servant to your King, though." When the Earl opened his mouth to correct her, she said, "Our King."

---

19 Typical titles for these servants would be Bailiff, Steward or Seneschal.

The Earl nodded.

"We are at my chambers, my lord," she said.

And they were, the wooden door guarded by two further men and firmly shut against their entry. Both the Countess and her new husband paused and looked at the door as if it might have the advice they required for whatever came next.

The Earl cracked first. "My lady, would you have your servants prepare alternative chambers for me?"

She let out a breath she hadn't realised she had been holding.

"You are still mourning the late Earl," said the newer one, "and it would be unseemly --"

A guard snorted.

"-- even less seemly to take his bed when his warmth has scarcely left it."[20]

The Countess forced another smile. "Oh, it is well known that the late Earl rarely warmed my bed, husband. I have no doubt my people are hoping you will prove to be a warmer man."

---

[20] It's unlikely that the Earl and Countess would have shared a chamber in any analogous period. But that would spoil the story.

And the Earl swallowed loudly.

"Peace, husband," the Countess said and her smile was genuine if cruel. "I will have someone prepare rooms for you."

The Earl nodded. "Thank you, my lady."

"But first we must enter my own rooms so that I can give the order," the Countess reminded him.

The door was pushed open by one of the guards, revealing three women waiting for the Countess's return.

"Come," said the Countess. "It will take some time. You may as well sit with me while we wait. Let me tell you an interesting story I heard."

The Tale of Blondel as told by the Countess

Blondel de Nesle is known to have composed at least twenty-four courtly songs. He was either Jean I de Nesle (c.1155-1202) or his son Jean II de Nesle (d.1241).

There was once a minstrel[21] so fair his own name was forgotten, and he became known as "Blondel" for his long, blond hair. His only ambition in life was to become the greatest musician who could and would use all of life in his songs. To this end, Blondel travelled to the Holy Lands as part of the Crusades[22].

It was in the Holy Lands that Blondel came to the attention of Lionheart[23], a man known for his

---

21 Blondel was a *trouvère* -- a Northern French word for a poet-composer like a troubadour -- and therefore an aristocratic noble rather than an itinerant musician.
22 Jean I took part in the Third Crusade (1189-1192). His son took part in both the Fourth Crusade (1202-1204) and the Albigensian Crusade (1209-1229).
23 Richard I of England was a leader of the Third Crusade, arriving in 1991. His use here suggests that the King of the main

love of beauty and fairness, as well as being something of a musician himself24. Blondel was much flattered by the attention and spent much time with his powerful new patron. The two worked on many compositions together, almost to the point of distracting Lionheart from his duties as King of England and leader of the Crusade. Many of his knights grew disquieted, perhaps even jealous of the attention. But the two continued in their partnership, singing love songs and composing their own tales of devotion.25

Despite his knights' complaints, Lionheart was still a great enough general that he won victory from the dust of the Holy Land by forcing the Unbelievers to allow True Christians to worship in Jerusalem.26 But when it was time to sail home for

---

story is not intended to be Richard I. Blondel was linked to Richard significantly after both men lived, although possibly before it was written down in 1260 as part of Récits d'un Ménestrel de Reims.
24 Richard may have considered himself a troubadour (trobador) as he was also a poet-composer but from the Southern French traditions.
25 Richard's sexuality doesn't seem to have been a point of discussion until the late Twentieth Century. The Countess would appear to have an opinion, however, and is making some very strong hints.

England the triumph of Jerusalem was soon forgotten for the captain of Lionheart's ship refused to take Blondel aboard for fear of bad luck at sea.27 The minstrel went from ship to ship, begging for any of the captains to take him so that he might follow his patron but not one would take him.

"My friend," Lionheart said as the two wept their goodbyes in private, "I shall never forget you."

That night, the two composed a short piece of two parts, with Blondel singing the plaintive verses that called out like hawk for its mate and Richard singing a triumphant answer as the refrain.

"I will follow you to the ends of the world," Blondel swore as he watched Lionheart sail away.

He began his march28 from the Holy Land as soon as the sails were out of sight, paying for his room and board with his songs.

---

26 This is a very bad summary of how the Third Crusade ended.
27 I have no idea why Blondel would be bad luck. It could just be he wasn't liked within the world of this story.
28 This is highly unlikely. Even if the real Blondel had been forced to travel over land, he would at least have had the funds to go by horse.

By the time he got to Constantinople, news reached Blondel that Lionheart had been kidnapped[29], his location hidden to prevent his rescue.[30] So Blondel composed a new plan to find his patron rather than to travel to England in the hopes of once more enjoying Lionheart's company. The very next day, Blondel began his new journey from Constantinople, intending to pass every castle in Christendom[31], singing the plaintive verses that only he knew and only Lionheart had heard. At every castle, Blondel walked away dejected when Lionheart

---

[29] Richard was taken prisoner just before Christmas 1192 near Vienna. He had offended the then Duke of Austria and probably arranged the murder of the Duke's cousin during the Crusade. Legend has it he was identified prior to capture by ordering expensive food or otherwise flashing the cash kings don't actually carry.

[30] This is very not true. Richard's location was very well known -- all of his prisons were very well defended, so they didn't need to be hidden. Also, he was being ransomed so making people doubt whether he was still alive would have been a very bad idea.

[31] Typically, Blondel only has to wander around the Holy Roman Empire or even just Germany. The Countess is being a bit harsh.

did not reply with the refrain that only he could sing.

Blondel made his way through Greece[32] from castle to castle and asked for any rumours of noble English prisoners at every place he rested. Rumour, however, did supply him with more news of Lionheart's kidnapping and he was able to straighten his path for the shores of Northern Italy[33] where Lionheart's ship had wrecked.

As Blondel walked, tales of him began to spread before and after him, of the mad minstrel who sang forlornly at castle walls. The tales spread so quickly that the soldiers within the castles began to wait for him, to call to him and throw stones at him when he sang beneath them.

"Be gone, mad man!"

"You sound like a drowning cat!"

"Hah! He sounds like a tom unable to get at a queen[34] in heat!"

More than once, he had buckets full of water thrown over him. Some were even cruel enough to

---

32 Strictly, the Byzantine Empire.
33 Part of the Holy Roman Empire at this time.
34 A female cat, not a human monarch or consort.

empty chamber pots on him.35 But the devoted Blondel continued to sing his love at the walls of every castle.

There were other rumours while Blondel walked, of lost Englishmen and alliances with French nobles36 but there was never enough detail for the minstrel to locate the grain of truth within them, never mind the mysterious Englishmen they were supposed to be about. But the number of them increased as the minstrel approached the Rhineland, so he took them as a sign from God to feed his hope.

After a year and a day of walking, Blondel came to the Rhenish town of Spires37 where he overheard a man in guard dress trying to recruit servants to serve a nobleman in a castle a day's travel away. The proposition made little sense to Blondel, although it is debatable whether the minstrel himself had any as he was so blinded by his devotion to Lionheart.

---
35 But, at least, he was never arrested or killed.
36 It's often alleged that the French King of the time (Philip II Augustus) encouraged Richard's kidnappers. He definitely offered to pay for Richard's continued incarceration.
37 Speyer in the Rhineland.

"Sir," he said to the guard.

The guard looked the ragged, somewhat dishevelled minstrel up and down.

"Why do you recruit so far from your own town? Are your own peasants so unwilling to serve your lord?" the minstrel asked.

His answer was a backwards swipe that bowled him over.

Blondel picked himself up and walked away but, as soon as he felt safe to do so, he found a place to sit and watch the recruiting guard. He did this rather than continue his way to the nearest castle and sing outside its walls as he had in every other place he'd been since leaving Constantinople.

"You there," the guard called to a young man. "You look a fine stout fellow capable of hard work."

The young man tried to walk away but the guard stopped him, holding out a silver coin. "There are more of these if you're looking for work."

The young man was tempted, fingers curling around the coin.

"I need a fine strong man that doesn't gossip," said the guard.

The watching Blondel sent a silent prayer to

God, thanking Him for his help.

"My lord has a fine guest who needs serving," the guard added, "who no doubt has coins of his own. If you play this right, you could have both paying you. If you keep your mouth shut."

The youth gave a close-lipped smile and the guard laughed.

"You'll do, my lad."

The coin was exchanged and Blondel quietly followed the two men from Spires. They led him to a castle on a hill and Blondel, hope rising in his heart like bird, could barely hold on to his song. It burst forth from him as if his call, his verse was the triumphant part.

There was quiet. There wasn't even the sound of guards disparaging the itinerant musician.

Blondel felt the bird in his heart dive into despair. He felt so lost that he could do nothing but collapse to the ground. God, it seemed, had not been behind him overhearing the guard's recruitment of a manservant.

He sang his part again, although flat with grief and despair.

Again, there was no reaction from the castle,

not even the insults and abuse Blondel had come to expect from inhabitants who knew nothing of his search for Lionheart. Although, when he listened, he thought he could hear metal clashing with metal. The inhabitants had no attention for him.

He cried enough that he could have filled barrels with his tears and then, when the tears were gone, he sang his part again. This time with he voiced the mourning cry of an animal that knows its mate has been lost forever.

And, this time, there was an answering refrain -- torn from an angry throat, the sound of an enraged bull or stallion that is being kept from its freedom. The words were unclear, but the tune and the intent were there.

"Lionheart!" Blondel cried out and sang a second verse, his notes rising to the triumph of his first rendition.

Before he had finished his verse, there was a scream and a man fell from a window. From the colours, Blondel recognised the fallen as a castle guard, but he couldn't tell whether it had been the one he'd followed.

Then Lionheart was singing again, a

triumphant stag on a German hill.

    Blondel cried out again, "Lionheart!" and then, "I have found you!"

    And he heard a cry of "Blondel!" back.

    The gates of the castle opened, and guards were hurrying towards Blondel. He considered being captured simply so that he could be with his patron once more but, in the end, prudence won, and the minstrel ran -- as far and fast as he could.

    Although he presumably stopped to eat and sleep, Blondel ran to Lionheart's mother[38], who had been gathering her son's ransom despite his subjects' lack of faith. Those most loyal to Lionheart who had survived the journey back to England from the Holy Land were among her entourage and they recognised the minstrel beneath his dirt and worn clothing.

    "Blondel," they snapped at him, "You'll find no patronage here. Your master has been taken by his enemies. Leave the real men to their work."

    But Blondel was insistent that they listen to him, repeating constantly "I know where Lionheart is; I have seen him!"

---

[38] Eleanor of Aquitaine.

Lionheart's mother, hearing this, asked, "Is this true?" and then, "Will those who doubt my son still lives believe this wild man?"

"In the Holy Land, he was known for composing music with Lionheart," said the loyal nobles. "He knows what Lionheart looks like and would not be fooled by a double."

So, Lionheart's mother used Blondel's evidence to prove her son alive and convince those who doubted his continued life to pay towards the ransom his captors had asked for. When the silver was transported, Blondel rode along with it as payment for his devotion and the first person to greet Lionheart in his freedom was his loyal minstrel.

Chapter Three: In which the Countess is offended

"I had heard that Blondel was actually the Lionheart's wife[39]," said the Earl in a flat tone. "I also thought the name Blondel was because he or she was the opposite of fair."

The Countess frowned.

"But it looks like my rooms have been made ready, so we should probably discuss this another day," said the Earl.

He rose from his seat on a stool at the Countess's feet. She hurriedly stood so that he was not looking down on her.

"But, my lord," she said.

"Good night, my lady," he said.

He hesitated for a moment before leaning forward to kiss her cheek. The Countess bowed her head so that he could not see her eyes. She did not watch him walk from her chambers. She did, however, throw her cup at the door after it had closed behind him.

---

[39] Berengaria of Navarre, and this was an idea put forward by poet Eleanor Anne Porden in 1822.

"A puppy!" she all but howled. "A puppy so enamoured of his king, he has no idea how to treat his wife!"

Her two lady's maids fluttered around her, hoping to calm her down but she was not to be soothed.

"I have only just rid myself of the last bore. Why must I be given another useless husband so soon? And the prince that keeps thrusting them at me is too busy with tournaments to hold his throne[40], never mind knowing what makes a good ruler."

She paced her chambers, unable to sit still or take up some distraction, until the maid who had overseen the preparation of the new Earl's rooms returned. This maid was not as attentive as the others. Indeed, she simply smiled at her mistress's discomfort and placed a hand on a belly beginning to round.

"Do not get too confident, wench," the Countess snarled at her. "My late husband's bastard

---

[40] This doesn't seem to correspond to any particular King of England as no-one has ever lost the crown due to tourneys but a number of them were fond of such stylised fighting.

has no rights to his estate-by-marriage while I and my blood live."

"A shame you have such difficulty finding husbands who will bed you, then," the former Mistress said.

The Countess would have thrown something again had she been able to get to something. However, her circling maids kept her from anything she might have picked up.

The Mistress said nothing.

"You are not my choice of lady-in-waiting," said the Countess. "Perhaps you should see about finding other employment."

The Mistress smiled more widely. "Perhaps you should see about finding servants who do not answer to the late Earl's true love."

The Mistress waved a hand as if to prove a point and the two lady's maids hurried from the room, leaving the Countess to pace in privacy. She heard them in the side-room she had assigned the unwanted lady-in-waiting when she had first arrived with the late Earl and their two sons, although the words held in their squawks and laughter did not make it through.

The Countess woke alone, without maids or lady-in-waiting let alone her unwanted new husband.

"I will have to bed him soon," she whispered to herself. "She has three fine sons and a fourth child on the way. If I do not bear children to this Earl, the people will look start to look to the children of the last."

The Countess rose and began to prepare herself for the day ahead. She could hear her maids chattering, tending the Mistress as if she were the true lady of the Isle of Ravens and not simply a lady-in-waiting.

"Or the bastards of the current one, if he can at least hold on to the title," said the Countess.

She snarled a little as her brush caught in her hair.

"Provided the superstitious peasants don't think marrying a widow a handful of weeks after her last husband died is not ill-starred."

The maids had fallen silent. The Countess fell silent, too, in case they heard her talking to herself.

"It was not my choice," she said when she heard normal morning sounds again from the Mistress's room. "I can hardly refuse the King."

After a few moments, she admitted, "I should have waited a longer time. Even if I am only mourning a toad of a man for form's sake."

It wasn't until she stood in as much finery and majesty as her rank and estate allowed that she added softly, "They will blame me."

Then, at a more normal volume, she called out, "Your lover did not trust you with matters of state or estate. You were an ignorant women kept only for his amusement. Now that he is no longer here to amuse, you should perhaps think of doing an honest day's work instead of biting the hand that could feed you."

The Countess sent a guard to invite her new husband to the Hall because the maids had ignored her until the moment she left her chambers. Then the Mistress walk beside her with insincere meekness, the two maids following behind like shadows.

The Countess seated herself at the head of the table. She smiled politely when the Earl arrived, led by the guard.

"Good morning, my lord," she said.

He bowed elegantly. "My lady."

"We should get you an esquire[41] and perhaps a couple of valets[42] to tend you," said the Countess.

The Earl sat close enough to the Countess that they could speak easily but far enough away that anyone who watched would think the two had no connection. She tried not to frown when she saw the Mistress, seated to her immediate left, cover a smile.

"I am used to tending myself except when arming myself for the fight," said the Earl.

"Yes," said the Countess, "but you are an Earl, now, not some Knight Errant on the tourney circuit."

---

41 A squire in the sense of someone who tends a knight and may or may not be a man-at-arms, although not necessarily someone who is training to become a knight and highly unlikely to be someone who owns the local manor (that would be a knight who has been well rewarded). The Countess is unlikely to accept anyone who isn't a fellow noble.
42 From the same root as varlet and used here to indicate a man servant similar to "a gentleman's gentleman".

The Earl nodded but said nothing.

"We have a status that we need to maintain," the Countess continued. "Our people expect it of us and others will lose their respect for us if we do not live up to these standards."

"Of course," the Earl murmured.

When breakfast was complete, the Earl stood and would have departed after bowing to the Countess but she held out her hand.

"My lord," she said.

The Earl stilled and looked at the outstretched hand as if it was a weapon that could cut his throat and flay the skin from his body with one move.

"My lord," the Countess said again. "It is time we introduced you to the business of being the Earl of this place, even if it is to be in name only."

The Earl stepped forward to take the hand and bow gracefully. "As you wish."

"No," said the Countess. "As the King wishes."

The Mistress frowned and beckoned one of the

maids forward. She whispered in the servant's ear and sent her away with a worried look. If the Countess noticed, she affected not to.

"You must become known here to more than the Chaplain. He's not held in high esteem43 and his word that you are my husband, even by the will of God and the King, will hold little weight," the Countess said.

"But your faithless words will?" the Mistress muttered.

The Earl looked from one woman to the other, unsure whether his new wife had heard her companion's venom and, if she had, why she would remain silent on the matter.

"You are not my choice," the Countess said and it was hard to tell who she was talking to, "but you are the one I must deal with."

The Earl nodded and said again, "As you wish."

"I do," said the Countess.

And the Earl smiled.

---

43 This in combination with the rarely used small chapel suggests that the Isle of Ravens would not be considered the mostly godly location.

"You think me funny?" the Countess asked.

He shook his head. "I find our situation so ridiculous that I do not believe it. If I were to tell someone of it, they would think I were telling a tale."

It was the Countess's turn to remain silent.

"There is something otherworldly about breaking my fast with a beautiful wife of large estate," the Earl said. "A poor knight rewarded with all the riches of fairyland for some good deed he cannot remember."

The Countess flushed and stuttered something that was almost thanks. The Mistress merely narrowed her eyes and held her tongue.

Chapter Four: In which the Earl begs leave

The Countess led her new husband around the Isle of Ravens, trailed by the Mistress, the two maids and a number of guards who kept those too low to exchange words with Earls and Countesses away. It became clear to the young Earl very quickly that all the other inhabitants of port were merchants, sailors, labourers, and their families.

Of course, it would be unseemly for nobles like the Countess and her new husband, or even her lady-in-waiting, to engage directly with any of these people but walking among them allowed the more important or self-important among the townspeople to wish them good morning and be introduced to their new Earl.

So, the party paced the town, accepted greetings from the most successful sea captains and merchants. They dutifully bowed their heads in the direction of the small chapel when the Chaplain walked by and made small talk with the Aldermen when they appeared with their chains of office.

"Are there no other knights or families of worth here?" the Earl asked the Countess in a moment of quiet.

"Are you too proud to meet with the people who pay for your existence?" she asked back.

The Earl stood on an embankment, part of the flood defences with ditches, fences and lock gates that only opened at low tide and stared out to the Abus, dark with silt and high with the Sea's tide. The protected stone quays sheltered ships and boats that were waiting for the next opportunity to leave but there were obviously plenty who were too impatient for that, an eagerness the Earl had not noticed when he had landed at night.

If the sheltered docks were a woody thicket made of masts, the waters just outside the defences were thick enough with more vessels to be mistaken for the greenwood. Determined merchants had built floating piers from walkways balanced on embankment-backed fences and walls. Labourers hurried with wheelbarrows laden with goods, back to warehouses a considerable distance away on solid ground. Sailors drew their ships in to the harbour formed by the curve of the spit-causeway that connected the Isle of Ravens to the mainland or withdrew from it as the passage of time required.

The air was heavy and full of all their activity. There was no doubting that this was a busy port and a considerable source of income.

"This is a port, a merchant town," the Earl said eventually. "I understand that everyone is here to increase the wealth of the city, but I would have thought the captain of your guard at least would be a knight rather than a man-at-arms[44]."

"Your predecessor had no problem with leading the guard[45] and you are a proven knight, are you not?" the Countess asked.

The Earl said, "I am."

---

44 Strictly speaking, a man-at-arms was a heavily armoured mounted soldier during the medieval to renaissance periods who may or may not have been of the noble classes. A knight is a type of man-at-arms, but a man-at-arms is not always a knight or a noble. The important point about them is that they would have been able to afford their arms, horse and heavy armour. The Earl probably means professional, peasant infantry soldiers and a semi-appropriate word has been attached.
45 It's unlikely an earl, his wife or their court would have really remained in one property year-round and thus long enough for him to effectively run the city guard. But this is a story, not reality.

And the Countess nodded briskly.

"Do you not visit your other properties?" asked the Earl.

The Countess gave a tight smile. "Surely you mean 'our properties'."

"No," said the Earl.

"One of us must always be here," said the Countess. "It is the jewel of my inheritance, the greatest gift my father left for me. It must be protected and held."

"Your other lands, your other people must be just as important, surely," the Earl said rather than asked.

And the Countess laughed.

"You disagree," he said in the same tone.

The Countess smiled and laid a consoling hand upon his arm. "You are young, husband. You have yet to learn so much of life's disappointments."

The Earl did not reply and the Countess removed her hand.

"Do not pretend you value the souls of our people any more than I do," she said. "I have seen you pay as little regard to the Chaplain and his chapel as the rest of us. I have seen no greater pull to God and prayer than I have in any of the merchants or guards or sailors."

The listening Mistress nodded and smiled quietly to herself. The Earl remained silent, although he nodded towards another approaching merchant in fine velvets and furs a noble would happily claim for their own.

The merchant's bow was low and obsequious, but his tone was that of one equal to another. "My lady. How pleasant to see you out in our fair town."

The Countess dipped her head slightly before turning to the Earl. Rather than introducing the two directly, she called the Earl "Husband," and talked of how many ships this merchant owned among the forest that docked in or by the island.

"The waters here are rich," was all the Earl said in response.

"Indeed," said the merchant, "and we happily supply the King[46] with the ten ships[47], and the

---

[46] It's unclear which King the merchant means: the true King who has recently sailed through or the usurper who presumably currently also holds the title.
[47] The most likely "real" the Isle of Ravens supplied one or two ships upon request, on several occasions, for

sailors to man them, he asks for."

The Earl looked at the masts. "I can see why. Ten would scarcely empty one quay."

The Countess frowned but the merchant smiled and nodded. "Indeed. The Isle of Ravens is second only to London in its wealth."[48]

The Earl murmured something about the floating piers.

"They *do* make trade less dependent on low tide," the merchant said, with another smile. "One of my captains had the idea."

"Do you need to dredge the berths?" the Earl asked.

The merchant paused.

The Countess replied, "The Abus tends to be thick with silt. You may have noticed the river-side of the causeway is starting to become another mud plain."

The Earl nodded.

The merchant said quietly, "Actually, I had

---

fighting Scots. The number given here is a significant exaggeration of wealth.
48 Not true of Ravenser Odd, the busiest port to have been situated in the Spurn Head area.

thought to ask you about that, my lady."

"To claim the land as fields? It will still be too wet to put anything on it[49] but I suppose we could look at extending the defences to protect them from high tide," said the Countess. "In our grandchildren's time, it may be usable."

"Not quite, my lady," said the merchant although he had nodded along when she'd spoken. "The porters are starting to grumble about how far they must move the goods from the piers."

"Oh?" asked the Countess.

"We, the other merchants and I, had thought we could use the dredged silt to fill the old docks within the defences. So that we may build warehouses closer to the fleet."

The Countess turned from the merchant, her face twisted into a deeper frown than ever. "Is there something wrong with the quays?"

"No, my lady," said the merchant, "but surely you see--"

"My wife and I will have to discuss this," said the Earl. "Such a change has risks as well as

---

[49] And salt-drenched. But both can be worked with to reclaim land from the sea.

benefits and we must understand them before we inflict them on our people."

The merchant bowed, "Of course, my lord," and backed away.

"You believe you have anything of weight to add to the discussion?" the Countess asked.

The Earl smiled. "Of course not. But you need time to consider it, not to be pressured into a quick decision because it is what one man wants."

The Countess did not seem any happier with this answer than she had without it. "Am I supposed to thank you?"

"No," said the Earl.

And he turned and walked away.

The Countess, determined to talk to him, was forced to follow him with her late husband's Mistress and the two maids trailing behind her.

"Then what do you expect?" the Countess demanded of her new husband.

"Nothing," he said, although he didn't stop walking. "Although you should use me as an excuse for delaying your decision."

"And how would you delay it?" asked the Countess.

"I won't be here to not discuss it with you," said the Earl.

"Ah, the puppy chases after its master, does it?" asked the Countess. "The King has sailed up the Abus and you will not catch him before the battle if you think to catch up with him on foot."

The Earl stopped as his feet touched the cobbles of the square before the Countess's palace. "You're assuming I haven't found a ship to take me after him."

The Mistress, hurrying behind the Countess as fast as her pregnancy would allow, gasped audibly.

"How?" asked the Countess and then she gave a bitter laugh. "You have not had time or opportunity to bribe a ship's captain."

"True," said the Earl.

The couple looked at each other while their attendants watched and waited.

The Earl said, "The King ordered me to hold the Isle of Ravens for him. I have no intention of abandoning his orders to join him in battle."

"Then what?" asked the Countess. "Why leave if you do not intend to chase your King? If he has ordered you to stay?"

The Earl shook his head. "He did not order me to stay, and I must leave for a few days to attend to my own business. It changes nothing here."

"You cannot," said the Countess.

"I will," said the Earl.

Chapter Five: In which the Earl returns

When the Countess sent one of her maids for the new Earl the next morning, the peasant returned ringing her hands and crying that the Earl was not there.

"What do you mean?" asked the Countess.

But it wasn't until the Mistress asked, "What is it, child?" that the maid answered.

"He is not there," the maid said. "The Earl is gone. And he's left a naked servant girl in his bed."

The Countess pursed her lips and asked, "Has he taken everything of his or does he mean to return?"

Again, the maid did not answer until the Mistress asked essentially the same question.

"His sword still hangs in its scabbard on the wall," the maid replied.

"Then he shall no doubt return in his own good time," said the Countess and she swiftly left her chambers to stalk her palace in search of the captain of her guard.

"Why did you not tell me the Earl had left?"

she demanded of the man-at-arms.

It was a while before he could answer, which he did with "I had no idea his lordship had left, my lady."

Upon being questioned, the guards that had stood watch outside his door expressed surprise at the Earl's absence. Those on shift at the time had noticed the servant girl enter early in the morning to light the fire in the Earl's chambers. A second pair of guards had been in place by the time the Countess's maid had come to the door and they swore they had seen the servant leave.

The servant girl herself, once woken, could only tearfully say, "He never did nothing, my lady, just said as I was looking tired that maybe I should take a lie-down and how he would never tell."

"And yet she woke without her clothes," the Mistress whispered, apparently to no-one as ladies do not gossip, but the maids heard and giggled.

The guards at the one gate on to the causeway denied having seen any sign of the Earl and if anyone on the quays and piers had seen him, they refused to admit it. No-one had seen anything out of the ordinary but the Earl had left, just as he had said he would have to.

Once again, the Countess said, "He will no doubt return in his own time."

And the Mistress whispered just loud enough for the two maids to hear, "If she keeps telling herself that, maybe she will believe it's true."

By the time night fell again, even the Countess had heard the other servants whispering about how her new husband would rather touch a peasant than his high-born wife and how he had escaped the unwanted marriage to join his beloved King on the battlefields of England.

"He has not," the Countess said to herself. "He promised his King and I believe him."

Separately, the Mistress said to the maids, "I wonder where the eager, young puppy has gone? I'll bet he has some love as young as himself he promised to marry and must now explain himself to."[50]

So, the next day, the Countess heard whispers of a feckless youth barely old enough to call himself a knight who had been gifted the unlovable

---

[50] The number of children she apparently arrived with would mean this is unlikely to be the Mistress's own origin story. She may be a bit bitter.

Countess when he really loved some younger, prettier daughter of another noble. Although, of course, he was not so in love that he hadn't been distracted by a pretty little servant, who he had seduced with his courtesy.

"It doesn't matter if he does," said the Countess to herself. "His King ordered that we marry and so we are stuck with each other."

"Unless the Usurper holds the throne," the Mistress whispered to the maids. "How quickly do you think these two will deny the connection, then? Everyone knows the Countess has no love for anything but money and the puppy clearly has no love of her."

Which became rumours that the Earl had gone to betray the true King to the Usurper so that he and the Countess might be free of each other, their marriage annulled, when the true King fell. The plan had, of course, been the Countess's because the Earl himself was too young and too naive to have formed such a plan himself.

And the Countess told herself, "He has not. He is far too devoted to his King to betray him."

The Mistress pursed her lips and let the maids' gossip between themselves. The Countess and

Earl the two described were of low enough morals without adding any more doubts to the situation.

    It was another three days before the Earl returned, attending the Countess at breakfast as if he had never been away.

    "You're back," she said. Then, almost too late to be observing form, "My lord."

    The Mistress watched intently, her hand freezing as she reached for food.

    The Earl bowed low over the Countess's hand. "I am, my lady."

    "Where have you been?" she asked.

    "It doesn't matter," he said.

    "You have duties here and you abandoned them," she said. "How can you tell me that it doesn't matter?"

    "I told you I had to go," said the Earl.

    The Countess stared at him. "And I told you you could not."

    "I am not a puppy to be ordered around," said the Earl. "I am a knight and your husband."

    "And?" asked the Countess.

    "And what?"

"If I do not tell you what you can and cannot do, how am I supposed to get you to behave?" she asked.

He stared back. "You could perhaps just trust that I know what I am doing and that I shall behave to the best of my ability."

"You are young and inexperienced," the Countess said. "You know nothing of being an Earl, of managing estates, of caring for our people."

The Mistress smiled and ate as if the finest banquet had been served instead of a simple breakfast51.

"Where have you been?" the Countess tried again. "What have you done? Why could you not stay here, where you are needed?"

"I needed to be elsewhere," said the Earl stiffly.

The Mistress asked, "Did you go to the King? Have you seen battle?"

"I promised him I would not," said the Earl. "And you are more likely to have heard any news than I. I have been to the North, while the King sailed

---

51 Given the era, their social status and the money involved, it's probably not butter on toast or a bowl of cereal.

south and west."52

      The Countess and the Earl each ate from their plates as if the other wasn't there and something like silence fell across the table. Only the Mistress seemed at all happy.

      "Has there been any news?" the Earl asked eventually.

      "No," said the Mistress.

      The Earl nodded.

      "Tell me where you have been," the Countess said.

      He ignored her.

      "Tell me what you have done," she said.

      He ignored her still.

      "Please," the Countess said. "Please tell me why you had to go."

      The Earl smiled and began to tell a story.

---

52 If the Isle of Ravens is based, however loosely, on Ravenser Odd, then the causeway leads to the north shore of the Abus / Humber. Although this scenario doesn't match against ether of the historical landings at Ravenser Odd, the King here is quite likely to have landed the second time somewhere on the southern shore, perhaps towards Winteringham where Ermine Street meets the river.

The Tale of Bisclavret as told by the Earl

Bisclavret was composed or retold by Marie de France, who was known to have written between 1160 and 1215. There is some debate about whether the name is simply a name or has a meaning that is probably a spoiler for what follows. For those who don't know, the alternative name for this tale is The Lay of The Werewolf.

There was once a Breton lord called Bisclavret who was much admired by his neighbours and a great friend to his king.53 As well as title, estate and office, Bisclavret held the hand of the fairest lady in Brittany. They loved each other, and only each other, from the day they met, and their marriage was considered the model of all other

---

53 The Earl has left out the introduction that explains about werewolves and how Bisclavret is not the usual sort. He presumably intends it to be a surprise for his wife -- and he is presumably drawing parallels with his own secret.

marriages in the kingdom. But, since the day of their marriage, there was a single problem that upset Bisclavret's lady so much that it was a struggle for her to have created that envied ideal, let alone maintain it.

Bisclavret had left her to her own devices on his estates two days into their young marriage and returned so full of cheer three days later that the lady almost doubted whether she was truly his only love. Mindful of her mother's advice the morning of the wedding, the lady bit her tongue and endeavoured to see beyond this incident. But Bisclavret left again several days later and, despite her gentle queries, no-one on the estates could tell her where her husband had gone.

The lady resolved to keep her disquiet to herself when Bisclavret returned and greeted his joyful content with her own welcoming cheer. She managed to maintain this cheer, or the appearance of it, for several years as Bisclavret for three days of every week that passed. Until there came a time when she could no longer hold her tongue or hide her true feelings about his disappearance.

"What is wrong, my love?" Bisclavret asked

when he saw her welcome was less warm than usual.

And the lady replied, "My husband, there is something I must ask you, but I am scared that the asking will upset you too much. Perhaps it is better not to know the answer than to risk your anger."

Bisclavret, caught up in the contentment and love that always filled him when he returned home to his beautiful wife, laughed, and took her in his arms.

"My love," he replied in between kisses, "you have no need to fear me. Ask me whatever you will."

The lady said, "I miss you when you are gone, my lord. It is as if you took my heart with you when you go and, from the moment you leave until the moment you return, I live in the fear that you will never return."54

"I will always return," Bisclavret promised.

"How can you promise me that?" asked his lady. "I have no idea where you go and what dangers you face. How can you promise me that when you might face enemies at every turn?"

"Just know that I will always return to you,

---

54 I have to question whether the Earl believes this love was sincere -- from either party involved.

my love," answered Bisclavret.

But his lady wasn't satisfied with that answer, and she demanded, "Why will you not tell me? I love you too much to cause you harm."

Bisclavret said softly, "If I tell you, you will stop loving me."

"That will never happen," said the lady. "You are my husband, the only one I love. How could I stop loving you?"

"Truly?" Bisclavret asked.

"I swear it," said the lady.

So Bisclavret told her why he left her company each week. "On the days when I am not here, I am a wolf in the Greenwood55. I live on whatever I can hunt and kill. There are none in the woods who could harm me."

The lady withdrew a little, knowing the tradition that werewolves are men who go mad and do whatever evil draws them, including eating other

---

55 The greenwood is not a true medieval concept, given the deforestation (in England) following the Norman Conquest. It's essentially a later, falsely nostalgic term that confuses forests (as in hunting park) with woodlands. This does not negate people running away to live in forests or woodlands.

men.

"You do not love me," said Bisclavret. "You doubt my honour too much."

And the lady stepped forward again. "Indeed, my love, I love you more. I know that you are a great man and that your soul is too good to allow your wolf-self to be so evil as other werewolves."

Bisclavret simply asked again, "Truly?"

"I swear it," said the lady.

Later, when the two of them lay in bed, the lady asked, "Do men go naked when they run as wolves?"

Bisclavret laughed. "As naked as the beasts we are."

"So, what happens to your clothes?" she asked.

"I put them somewhere safe," Bisclavret said but he refused to answer any further questions.

Over their breakfast, the lady asked, "But where do you put your clothes? You must put them for safe keeping for you to return in such good order."

"By the old chapel," said Bisclavret.

"Surely not out in the open where anyone might see them," said the lady. "There is no place out of sight in those ruins."

"The old font has been overturned and is now hidden by the undergrowth," said Bisclavret.

"It is a shame it is too late to donate money to the chapel," said the lady. "I would give all I had in thanks for your safe-keeping and protection."

Bisclavret laughed and kissed her. "My safe-keeping and protection depends on you, not an ancient chapel. If anyone steals my clothes, they curse me to be a werewolf for the rest of my days."

"I love you more than anything or anyone," said the lady. "I have no desire to lose you. You can trust me."

However, when Bisclavret went out into the greenwood again, his lady called upon a neighbour who had once courted her.

"My friend," the lady, who had previously rejected his affections, said, "My heart is yours and I am only ashamed that I never admitted it sooner."

The knight was not so honourable that he could refuse the lady's body and he didn't think to ask until afterwards why she would offer it now.

"My lord has revealed his true self," said

the lady. "He hunts the greenwood as a werewolf."

"And I will hunt the werewolf," the knight swore.56

So the lady told her new lover of Bisclavret's hiding spot, and how her husband would be there in two days' time to collect his clothes and return to his human life.

The knight followed the lady's directions but, too impatient to wait there for two days, he simply took Bisclavret's clothes. On his own estate, he cut the clothes and stained them with an animal's blood before returning to the lady's side at the appointed time.

Bsclavret, of course, did not return -- just as his fearful wife had planned, although not because he was dead. After a week of absence, the lady had the knight lead search parties, and these parties roamed the area for weeks. After several months, Bisclavret's other family and friends were -- in their ignorance of his werewolf form --- discouraged enough to declare him dead. After a year, Bisclavret's estates and the neighbour knights

---

56 This is not exactly what happens in Marie de France's version.

were united when the lady married her lover.

The king attended the lady's second wedding and, shortly after the ceremony, was hunting in the greenwood thereabouts. His host, the knight, did not accompany him due to estate business but had the hunting party guided by the former servants of Bisclavret who knew the area well.

The hounds ran backwards and forwards through the woods and eventually found Bisclavret's scent. As is the way with hunting hounds, the recognised the werewolf-scent only as prey, if only because the only human that they knew to be their leader was their keeper. They flushed the confused Bisclavret from the undergrowth and, with the huntsman sounding his horn, pursued him across his own estates.

After a day of being pursued, the torn and bloodied Bisclavret chanced to double back on the hunting party and found himself staring at the king he had served so loyally before. Desperate, and possibly unknowing of all that had gone before his life in the greenwood, the werewolf threw himself at the king, clutching a stirrup between his paws and licking the boot of his former master.

Despite his fear of the strange wolf, the

king called his hunting companions to him. "My lords! Look at this beast with the sense of a man! How can we harm this wonder?"

So, the hunters called and beat their hounds from their quarry, declaring this the end of the hunt. But Bisclavret refused to leave the king's side so he followed them back to a nearby lodge. He spent each moment of that evening at his master's feet, only accepting food from the king's own hand and only sleeping at the bottom of the king's own bed.

The king was so taken with the beast, unaware of its true history, that he allowed the beast to keep its place at his side. Feeding the werewolf by hand amused him endlessly and having the weight at the end of his bed stilled any fears the king had of Bisclavret's former neighbours and servants, doubted since his loyal servant's disappearance.

So, the two continued to lead the hunt for another week before the king could accept that he must return to his duties and the werewolf must either stay a wolf in the greenwood or become a man in the court.57

---

57 Again, not exactly how Marie de France

The king demanded clothing be brought for his werewolf servant and laid out before it. But Bisclavret acted as if the clothes were not there.

"You cannot be a beast at court," said the king.

But Bisclavret stepped on the velvets and linens as if they weren't there.

"Your majesty," said a hunting companion, "perhaps the poor beast is embarrassed to admit who he truly is. Or he may have been a beast so long that he knows nothing of the world."

The king eventually agreed. "I think you are right. I shall have to leave my new companion behind."

And the hunting party prepared to leave but, again, Bisclavret refused to leave the king's side. He even ran alongside the king's horse as the party returned to Bisclavret's former home from the hunting lodge.

The treacherous knight who had married Bisclavret's former lady recognised the werewolf that ran beside the hunting party and closed the gates against them.

---

tells it. The Earl is making a point.

"Why have you closed the gate against me?" the king asked. "Why would a loyal vassal block his king's way?"

The knight replied, "I am sorry, your majesty, but I cannot allow you to enter while that beast accompanies you. The sight of it would scare my gentle wife."[58]

"Come and open the gate," the king and his companions insisted.

The knight refused again.

"Open the gate," said the king, "or I shall have you tried for treason."

This time, the knight could not refuse, and he opened the gate himself. However, as soon as Bisclavret caught sight and wind of him, the werewolf threw himself at the throat of his former lady's husband. The hunting companions barely managed to separate the two.

"You know this werewolf," the king said, certain of it.

"No," said the knight, "I swear it."

But he kept as far from the snarling werewolf

---

[58] And presumably give away the fact that her second husband had been too lazy to actually do as she'd asked.

as courtesy would allow, given that Bisclavret refused to leave the king's side. The king, in his turn, asked that a leash be brought for the werewolf so that ladies need not be scared of him.

In the hall, the lady greeted the returned hunting party -- and screamed at the sight of the werewolf prowling by the king's side. Bisclavret, already on edge in the presence of the knight, would have attacked the lady if he had not already been tied.

"You recognise this werewolf," the king said.

But the lady's sight was on Bisclavret and her words were aimed at her knight. "You said that you had killed him."[59]

The knight did not answer.

"You said that you had killed him," she said again. "Yet here he is, a werewolf in my home."

"What do you mean?" the king asked.

And the lady, knowing she was caught, said. "This is my former husband, Bisclavret."

"The one you thought missing?" asked the king.

---

59 In Marie de France's version, torture is required to get a confession. The Earl is a far kinder story-teller.

"The one I thought dead," she corrected. "Killed by the hand of this knight."

The knight said, "She told me to steal his clothes while he was a werewolf and kill him before he became a man again."

"And you do everything another's wife tells you, do you?" the king asked.

The king had Bisclavret taken to his chambers and left with his own clothing. Eventually, Bisclavret returned, a lord and knight again, clothed appropriately.

"Your majesty," he said, bowing deeply over his master's hands.

"My friend," said the king, hugging his lost companion. "I cannot bear to think of the crimes committed against you."

But Bisclavret said, "Everything that was done was done due to fear."

"You are a most noble and forgiving beast," said the King.

So Bisclavret was returned to his estates and gained his former neighbours, while the false lady and her second husband were driven from the land to make a new future of their own.

Chapter Six: In which a marriage is made

"You were away for a week, not three days," said the Countess.

The Earl nodded.

"Are you telling me that you will be gone again in as many days?" she asked. "Or sooner?"

"Are you telling us that you're a werewolf?" the Mistress asked.

The Countess glared. "There are no such things as werewolves or men who become wolves. The Church tells us that to believe in them is a heresy."[60]

"And you care what the Church thinks?" asked the Mistress.

When the Countess would have answered her, the Earl said quietly, as if the mistress had not spoken, "No. Well, probably not."

"'Probably?'" the Countess asked.

---

[60] This was true of witches and the early to mid-medieval Church -- to the point where people who raised the issue of prosecuting others for witchcraft were pointedly asked if they wanted to be tried for heresy.

"The business that calls me away is generally once a month," said the Earl. "So, it will call me from you in three weeks. Unless I hear otherwise."

"Your business is here," said the Countess. "You are my husband. We have an estate and people to take care of."

"And I do. I will," said the Earl.

The Countess said, "It would be easier if you gave up these other interests."

"This is something I cannot avoid," said the Earl.

"May I remind you that we are expected to have heirs in due course," said the Countess. "Something that will be difficult if you are spending most of your time somewhere else."

"With someone else?" asked the Mistress.

Husband and wife ignored her.

"That is a matter we must discuss another time and not in front of servants," said the Earl.

"I am not a servant," said the Mistress.

Husband and wife continued to ignore her.

The Earl said softly, "You have only recently been widowed and I would have rather given you time to mourn your late husband properly. This is the best that I can do."

"There is not much to mourn," said the Countess, and the Mistress gasped in response. "But your kindness is appreciated."

"That's not how it seemed on your wedding night," the Mistress muttered.

"It is the King's order that I hold this place in his name but you hold it well enough on your own," said the Earl. "I will support you in every way I can -- and that is all that my duties to you and him require of me."

"You can support me by not disappearing to God knows where," said the Countess.

And the Earl shook his head. "I must attend to my own business. I will try to keep it brief, but it is inescapable."

"Then tell me what it is," said the Countess.

The Earl replied, "'Just know that I will always return to you, my love.'"

Exasperated, the Countess pushed what remained of her meal aside and left. She paused for a moment in the doorway and turned to the Mistress.

"Are you really so impudent that you no longer serve me at all?" she asked the Mistress and her maids.

The maids exchanged looks but made no move until the Mistress herself stood and languidly followed the Countess, who swore an oath before sweeping out completely. The Earl stared after the four women for a while before sighing and returning to his own meal.

"I never intended to marry," he said aloud. There were guards by the door who heard him, but they were out of both his sight and mind. He spoke without thought of an audience. "I wanted only to be a knight in service to my king or competing at the lists."

There was silence for a while and then the Earl whispered, too quietly to even hear the word himself, "Children."

His laughter sounded like a rough bark.

"Children," he said again.

The Earl kept his word and supported his wife in everything. On each occasion that he was approached while on his own to discuss matters of the estate, he gracefully deflected demands for an answer and promised to discuss the matter with the

Countess. When raising these matters, he did not demand that his view become the order but accepted her ruling. He never asked that she explain herself. He never presented her orders as anything but her decision.

"Why?" she asked him.

He replied, "This is your city, and you know it far better than I do or ever will."[61]

"It is not yet a city," the Countess said and she smiled. "It will be in time. Perhaps in our children's time or their children's time."[62]

Beside them and ignored, the Mistress cupped her hands around her rounding belly and whispered something they didn't hear to herself and the child within.

So, the Countess's decisions were those that ruled the port and the people who sheltered there in the mouth of the mighty river Abus, though the

---

[61] Flattery gets you... a slightly happier wife.

[62] Aside from the assumptions about her family's future, the Countess is forecasting a lot of growth for a town that is probably not much more than a fishing port in terms of the goods it handles -- although the first along the river.

merchants and aldermen still came first to the Earl as if he might, somehow, change his own mind and rule without his wife's opinion.

"The King has at least given you a good puppy," the Mistress said to the Countess. "So well trained and obedient to another's command."

The Countess replied, "I wouldn't say that. He will be leaving to go about his own business in a matter of days."

But she later she asked herself, "Is he too soft? Too weak? Would a stronger man make a better Earl?"

At the same time, the Mistress smiled to herself and told her barely observable pregnancy, "He is not the man your father was. Your blood and your brothers' will be better suited than his children's."

But the Mistress was not content with this and shared the doubts the Countess had expressed with the maids, framing her gossip as concern for her former rival's position now that she had been pushed into such a poor marriage.

"Because," she said to the maids, "if the people of Ravens' Isle take against the Countess and her puppy of a husband, they are likely to take against the whole household."

It didn't take long for the words to spread around the town and the next burgher[63] who approached the Earl refused to accept his promises to discuss the matter with the Countess.

"Are you not a man, then?" asked the burgher. "Are you a child that a woman must make all your decisions for you? Or a dog that can only do as its master or mistress tells it?"

The Earl forced a smile. "I am simply a knight. My lady the Countess is more familiar with the issues you face than I am."

"You are the lord of this place," said the burgher.

"By virtue of my marriage," said the Earl. "And any man of sense knows that a marriage cannot be happy if his wife is not consulted on the things

---

63 A burgher is a freeman (i.e. not owing feudal service to anyone, just taxes) of a town, particularly a fortified town. The Isle of Ravens isn't, strictly speaking, one of these despite having walls. It is presumably used here so the storyteller can be vague about

that concern her happiness."

"You're no use to man nor beast," the burgher spat.

The Earl shrugged. "My lady and I will discuss the matter you raised, and I will make your argument to her. If the argument is a good one, she will no doubt decide in your favour."

"Don't bother," said the burgher. "I'll make the argument myself when I am granted a hearing."

The Earl watched the burgher stalk away, swearing.

"And yet," said the Earl, "they think it worthwhile to talk to wives and mistresses of noblemen in the hopes that the lords' hearts will be softened by their bed mate's words."

He said the same to the Countess at the dining table and the Mistress laughed aloud.

"But you aren't her bed mate," one of the maids said and then covered her mouth as if she would be punished for speaking.

No-one reacted as if they had heard her.

"They have little faith in the King," said the Countess. "They do not realise that he would not leave a soft, weak man behind to hold an important port. A knight would not compete in tourneys if he were incapable."

"This is not about my capabilities with a sword or lance," said the Earl.

"No," agreed the Countess.

The Mistress smiled placidly.

"They will learn in time," said the Countess. "Or they would if they heard how you argued their cases or saw how quickly you had learnt the skills of managing the estate."

And her no longer quite so new husband nodded slowly.

"Stay," said the Countess. "Don't go"

"I must," said the Earl.

Chapter Seven: In which the Earl runs away a second time

The Earl pretended to sleep while a servant girl woke a flame from the glowing embers of the previous day's fire. He waited patiently while she worked, and he heard the multiple footsteps that came with the changing of the guards stood at his door. He kept his breathing even while she came to peer at him in his bed and muttered something about him being too young and pretty for the heartless Countess. He kept still while she walked from the room to repeat the same task in said Countess's own chambers.

"I wish she hadn't increased the guard," the Earl said to himself when he thought it safe.

The marching footsteps had been enough for four men rather than the usual half-hearted two.

"She has been counting days and watching me," he said. "She doesn't trust that my business is harmless."

He rose and stripped off his night-shirt.

He sighed and asked, "Who can blame her?"

Then he stripped away the cloth that bound his chest.

The night-shirt he left somewhere obvious but the binding cloth he piled with the clothes the maid had placed at the end of the bed. He hid the pile in the bottom of a trunk that had been there when he'd first arrived, and no-one had thought to search when he had last run away. From the same trunk, he took the clothes he had stolen from the previous servant girl, a bundle of rags and a scarf to wrap around his short hair.

"I would prefer to walk from here as the Earl, but she will not let me," he said. "At least a servant girl may walk wherever people are too blind to see or care."

He left his arms and armour, save for a dagger, where they could be seen -- "my promise as a knight that I will return" -- and left his chambers in a close approximation of the last serving girl's gait. He gave an embarrassed giggle as the four guards looked at him and scurried away before any of them managed to talk at him.

"Young'un's not as innocent as he looks, then," one of them said.

The Earl heard the four of them laughing after the servant girl they thought they'd seen leaving his chambers.

"I'm sorry," he whispered.

But he wasn't sorry enough to return to his chambers instead of walking straight out of the palace by the servants' entrance. Or to turn aside at the turnpike64 at the beginning of the causeway back to true land.

The Earl, as a servant girl, was not questioned about his movements but the guards at the turnpike did watch him walk past and comment on the comely maid. The Earl flushed and hurried his steps.

He was not the only person on the causeway, but he was the only person travelling to the mainland. Almost everyone else was transporting foodstuffs65 and water66 to the Isle of Ravens while

---

64 "Turnpike" first crops up as a word in the English language during the 15th Century, when it indicated a type of spiked barrier used to block a road for defensive purposes. It eventually became a type of toll gate, somewhat later than this story is supposed to be set. In this instance, it probably means a simple guarded gate not dissimilar to the simple barriers we see at a car-park.
65 Although there are a number of reclaimed fields alongside the causeway, it's unlikely that the Isle

he was hurrying away.

A wagoner stopped him. "Where are you going, girl?"

"Does it matter?" he asked.

"You are too pretty to be so sour," said the wagoner. "Smile, girl."

"I am not pretty," said the Earl but he kept his hands, scarred, and calloused from learning to fight, hidden in the stolen skirts.

"You're pretty to me," said the wagoner. "Won't you be nice and smile for me?"

The Earl turned his face away as he shook his head. He didn't stay to hear any more but hurried on as fast as he could without breaking into a run.

"Miserable bitch!" the wagoner called after

---

of Ravens, or any actual settlement at the end of Spurn Head (or older versions), could produce its own grain, fruit and vegetables. It's possible that there would be some animal husbandry in the drier months but not enough to support the entire port.

66 The groundwater at the Isle of Ravens would likely be brackish, if not outright seawater, given that the port (or real equivalent) is built on a sand bar. With the causeway, water can be transported by wagon as well as by ship.

him.

When the Earl did not pause or turn back, the wagoner yelled more loudly, "You're ugly anyway and I was only taking pity on you!"

"If I were myself, I could have you dragged before the court," the Earl muttered to himself. "If I were myself, I could have run you through for your insolence."

But the Earl could only clench his fists and walk along the causeway and then, once the causeway reached the mainland, along the King's Road. His wife's lands and estate became rolling and green, lush with growth and carefully tended by her vassals. He avoided them as much as the road allowed, head down and steps hurried.

The Earl did not slow until he came to a wasteland[67] where the Greenwood had begun to

---

[67] In medieval terms, wasteland is countryside that is not tended and farmed in some way, not necessarily a place where nothing lives. In the British Isles, wastelands were usually this way because a village died through some sort of disease or possibly violence. Otherwise disappeared settlements, such as those destroyed by the Highland Clearances, did not become wastelands as their human inhabitants

encroach on the ruins of a stone church and the land was humped in a way that indicated the buried remains of less rugged houses. Large enough to hold ten of the Ravens' Isle chapel, the church's stone walls still held up a sagging slate roof. But some of the slates had fallen and undergrowth poked through where windows should have been.

"This must be the edge of my lady's lands," the Earl muttered. "I never thought to ask when I returned last time."

He crept through the arched entrance where a door should hang and made his way to the vestry he knew to remain relatively whole.

"But if I'd asked, she would have known where to find me," he said. "For I'm sure that even if this village was never hers, she knows of it."68

---

    were simply dispersed to allow more profitable use of the land, such as sheep grazing or hunting parks.
68 A large church means this is very likely the remains of a large village or possibly even a town. Which means that the Countess <u>should</u> have heard of it. It's quite likely that there would be local folklore about it. However, it doesn't have any obvious parallel in real life and may only exist for narrative purposes.

But as he pushed open the grey remains of a wooden door, the Earl froze.

The vestry was a Greenwood scene, several yeomen69 resting in the shelter of bushes that had broken through the stone of the church. One among the yeomen lay beneath the branches of the tallest of the undergrowth, his head sheltered on the lap of a fair maid. To one side, another yeoman strummed a small harp and sang along, too quietly for the words to be clearly heard. There was an array of bows and short swords, even by the maid.

Then there was silence as everyone turned to look at the Earl. He reached for his own sword -- despite it being hung on a wall a day's travel away and not at his side.

"I am sorry for disturbing you," he said. "I didn't realise anyone else was here."

The one who was lain across the maid's lap pushed himself up on an elbow. "Who are you, girl?"

"Are you Robin Hood70?" asked the Earl. "And

---

69 From how this setting works, yeoman here can be considered a peasant military class with relatively light arms and leather and / or mail armour.
70 Robin Hood, as a ballad character, dates from 1377 at the latest as he's

Maid Marian[71]? And Allan-A-Dale[72]?"

The yeoman who had spoken frowned. "How old do you think I am?"

The yeoman with the harp laughed softly.

The maid whispered to her companion, and he laughed, the frown easing, before saying aloud, "I am John Barleycorn[73], and this is my girl, Dolly.[74] These are my men."

---

mentioned in Piers Ploughman.
71 Maid Marian was a May Day tradition that became associated with Robin Hood by the 16th Century.
72 Allan-a-Dale was first associated with Robin Hood in a Child Ballad dated to the 17th century.
73 John Barleycorn is a folkloric embodiment of barley and alcoholic drinks made from the grain. He may be the conceptual descendent of a Northern Germanic character named Beowa ("Barley"). It's difficult to date the folk-songs associated with John Barleycorn but the first known poem was published in 1568.
74 This is presumably a joke about corn dollies, an item woven from the last stalks harvested in a given community. This would be a home for the spirit of the grain's spirit over winter and then it would be ploughed into the field in spring so that it would become the crop-to-come.

Chapter Eight: In which words are exchanged

"Who are you, girl?" John Barleycorn asked again.

"I--" began the Earl.

But the yeoman with the harp interrupted with, "It's a little unfair to ask a lady her name in a place where given names remain unknown."

"I don't understand," the Earl said.

"Oh?" asked Dolly. "Do you think this man is really called 'John Barleycorn', then?"

The Earl didn't answer.

"Too Norman or Breton to know who John Barleycorn is, no doubt," the yeoman in question said. "Like you, dear heart and daughter."

Dolly snapped her teeth at him.

"What name do you wish to be known by?" asked the yeoman with the harp. "What is your role in the story you find yourself in?"

"I am the Earl," said the Earl.

And the gathered yeomen laughed.

When the Earl did not join the laughter, John Barleycorn wiped the water from his cheeks and said, "Sorry. I thought you were joking."

"The title is not a responsibility I ever wanted," said the Earl. "It's not something I would joke about."

John Barleycorn laughed again.

Dolly, however, elbowed him and replied gently, "Of course not."

"You don't look like an Earl," said the yeoman with the harp.

The Earl looked down at the stolen skirts. "I am in disguise."

"Funny," said John Barleycorn. "The disguise fits so well; I would say you were born to it."

"It's a mask I have worn for most of my life, but is just a mask," the Earl said.

He gripped the bundle of rags he had carried with him from the Isle of Ravens and waited.

"You don't behave like a noble," said John Barleycorn. "You haven't shouted orders or treated us with disdain."

And, again, Dolly elbowed him. He laughed, again, and grabbed her hand. She simply glowered at him.

"You must forgive our leader and his girl," said the yeoman with the harp. "If it were a marriage instead of an adoption, we would call it one of convenience."

"I am familiar with the concept," said the Earl.

The yeoman finally introduced himself, "I am Hugh75."

"A pleasure to meet you," said the Earl. "What are you all doing here?"

"Roaming the Greenwood, gathering stories," said Hugh.

"So, if I tell you a story, you will leave me alone?" asked the Earl.

John Barleycorn said, "Not what we had in mind, but why not?"

"And you'll leave this church so I may have some peace?" asked the Earl.

"And there it is," said John Barleycorn. "The noble. Expecting the world to account for their whims."

---

75 Hugh is the Anglophone version of a Germanic name, despite the modern Welsh associations. The starting element, hug, has something to with the mind or spirit. It is, coincidentally, probably the name of a Midlands poet responsible for writing down Sr Gawain And The Green Knight and a few other poems.

"I need to be alone for a few days," said the Earl.

Dolly muttered, "I understand that feeling."

"Yes," said John Barleycorn to her, "but you're not capable of looking after yourself."

Dolly hissed at him.

"Too much noble blood," he added.

The Earl said to Hugh, "Their relationship does not seem very convenient to anybody."

Hugh smiled. "Very true."

"I need to shelter here," the Earl said to Hugh, "for a few days. I will be gone within a week. But I cannot be around others."

"Why? Do you turn into a werewolf?" asked John Barleycorn.

"No," said the Earl. "Only someone who will kill a fool rather than suffer them gladly."

"Another short-tempered woman," John Barleycorn replied.

"Perhaps you should consider the cause of their temper before making such pronouncements,"[76] said the Earl.

---

[76] Often rendered "If all of your exes are crazy, it's time to look at the common denominator."

"No," said Dolly.

"No?" asked John Barleycorn.

"No, we will not leave if... the Earl tells us a story," said Dolly. "However, we will let... him stay here in peace and quiet."

The Earl said, "How will I have peace and quiet if you're all in the vestry with me?"

"We can move to the nave," said Dolly. "We have more friends coming, anyway, and this room will be too small for all of us."

"More?" asked the Earl.

"This is not the whole company77," said John Barleycorn.

The Earl stared at the yeomen's leader. "And why are you here? Should you not be fighting? Or has the King regained his throne?"

"We have served our king and been forgotten," said John Barleycorn.

"Several times," added Hugh.

"Our home is the Greenwood and that is all

---

77 This is used in the military sense of a group of soldiers under a leader not a collection of people working for a business. Although fighting people is as much a business as any other.

that matters," said Dolly.

The Earl stared. "All that matters?"

"If your king is so important to you, why are you not fighting for him?" asked John Barleycorn.

"Our king," said the Earl. "He is our king."

John Barleycorn laughed. "He is the King of England, I grant you, but so the other could be, too. It doesn't matter to the Greenwood who wins or holds the throne. And none of that explains why his good... Earl is here when he needs help."

"You laugh too much over matters you know nothing off, John Barleycorn," said the Earl.

"It matters," said Hugh. "Have we not already learnt that?"

John Barleycorn shrugged. "The two that fight are brothers. Their blood is equally good, even if one does look like a Saracen78."

"The King is as Christian as you or I," said the Earl.

---

78 The word Saracen began its life as a Greek and Latin term to refer to desert tribes around the Roman province of Arabia who weren't actually Arabs. Arabs were lumped in with them under the same term from the early Middle Ages and it eventually became a catch all for Muslims.

"Which is not very much, then," said John Barleycorn.79

The Earl glared.

"You talk too much, John," said Dolly, "and your words are too sharp edged."

John Barleycorn snorted at her.

"One day you will cut yourself," she said quietly.

"But my darling girl will always be there to tend my wounds," said John Barleycorn.

"If I must put up with your presence," said the Earl, "then I expect more for the price of a story than space to sleep in the vestry."

It was Hugh that laughed this time. "This must be a good story, then."

"What did you have in mind, girl?" asked John Barleycorn.

"I am informed that an earl requires an esquire and possibly even valets to attend him," said the Earl. "My wife has been telling me so for the last month."

---

79 Well, they are all arguing about camping out in a ruined church. There's got to be an element of desecration in there.

"Your wife?" laughed John Barleycorn.

"Somehow I doubt John would make a decent valet," said Dolly. "He's far too bitter and coarse to serve as a noble's companion."

"I was hoping he would be my esquire. He would certainly annoy my wife's lady-in-waiting no end," said the Earl.

"But not your wife?" asked Dolly.

The Earl smiled. "My wife is too annoyed by me to notice his existence as anything more than my servant. His behaviour will reflect on me, not him."

"And is Dolly to be your valet?" John Barleycorn asked.

"No," said the Earl. "One of your men, perhaps, but not Dolly. My wife could do with a servant she can trust. Dolly can be her maid or a second lady-in-waiting. Whichever my wife thinks her suitable for. Are you of noble birth?"

Dolly shook her head. "Just a noble's bastard."

"And you think that you can trust us?" asked John Barleycorn.

"To behave? No," said the Earl. "To be yourselves? Yes."

"I will be your valet," said Hugh.

John Barleycorn stared at him. "What?"

Hugh replied, "I would like to know how this story ends. I would happily play the valet to hear it."

"I haven't started telling it, yet," said the Earl.

"Oh," said Hugh. "Not that story. The one you're in."

John Barleycorn stood and paced the vestry. Where they were unfortunate enough to be in his way, the other yeomen hurriedly but quietly moved. Dolly remained where she had always been.

"For how long?" asked John Barleycorn.

"How long do you intend to be in the area?" replied the Earl.

John Barleycorn shrugged. "For as long as we feel like it. For as long as this part of the Greenwood can support us."

The Earl nodded and said nothing.

"For a year and a day," suggested Hugh. "It is, after all, traditional."

"Or until I ask you to leave," said the Earl.

"Tell your story." Said John Barleycorn, "and

I will tell you if I agree to your terms."

The Earl shook his head. "And if you don't agree? What then? I will already have told you the story."

"Then we will find somewhere else to shelter and leave you the church to yourself," said Dolly.

John Barleycorn glared at her but held his hand out to the Earl. "Deal?"

The Earl took the offered hand and shook it. "Deal."

The Tale of The Loathly Lady as told by the Earl

"loathly" - "More modern English would be "ugly" or "loathsome". The whole phrase could also be the old fashioned "shrew", as in the taming thereof

There was once a white hart[80] and, as everyone knows is the purpose of such creatures, it was a prize most desired by every noble man in the country. King Arthur himself hunted this beast and brought it to bay with his hounds. He would have slain it for the many-tined antlers if his hounds had not been beaten back by a heavily armoured man with a club.

"Sir," Arthur called out, "why do you mistreat my hounds in this manner?"

But the armoured man ignored the king and continued to lay into the hounds. The hart, no longer the focus of attention, escaped.

Now, King Arthur was not hunting alone, for kings are too valuable to be left unattended and

---

[80] Another archaic word, this time for a mature stag.

there were many knights with him. Among them was his young nephew, Gawain, who had not yet attained his full strength, or learning, or courtesy. In all, Gawain was as fair a young fool as any man who lived and enraged at the slight to his uncle, he charged the armoured man.[81]

The foolish boy had a measure of success[82], throwing the armoured man to the ground so hard that the man could not even respond, let alone continue to beat the hounds with his club.

"My uncle asked you a question, wretch!" Gawain shouted.

And the armoured man cursed him.

Gawain gave the man another buffet and said, "Speak with a civil tongue, you oaf, and answer my uncle. Why do you mistreat his hounds?"

"Why does your uncle hunt on lands that are rightfully mine?" asked the armoured man. "And why do you, no more than a pup, treat a knight of the

---

[81] This set-up differs significantly from the more familiar "The Wedding of Sir Gawain and Dame Ragnelle" (written in the 15th Century) or the similar "The Marriage of Sir Gawain" (collected in the 20th Century).

[82] I'm pretty sure the Earl identifies with Gawain.

realm with such contempt and discourtesy?"

"Who are you?" asked King Arthur but before the man answered he said, "Gawain, help him up."

Gawain did as his uncle and king commanded, though he looked sour with it, and helped the armoured man to his feet. The man still did not answer any of the questions.

"Who are you?" King Arthur asked again.

The man removed his helm to reveal a striking, sharp face. "I am Sir Rummer Summerday[83], the lord of this wood[84], and you have wronged me, and your nephew has wronged me. I demand satisfaction."

"I had thought that Arthur, King of the Britons, was lord of this place," said King Arthur.

"You are not," said Sir Rummer, "And you know it. For your hunt has brought you to the Greenwood

---

[83] The knight's name is usually given as Sir Gromer Somer Joure.
[84] If it had been a true forest (i.e. hunting ground), Arthur would have been hunting with the lord or his permission. It's likely that this knight is something more Otherworldy. Oddly, the Earl has not describe him as a Green Knight, which is the usual way of conveying this.

and your quarry was the finest of my cattle, my good white bull."

The hunting part, including King Arthur, drew back in fear for the armoured man could only be an elf knight to speak so. But Gawain, young and inexperienced, remained where he was by Sir Rummer.85

"Your fine, white bull is safe since you interrupted the hunt," said Gawain.

"He is scarred and weary. So weary that he may not be strong enough to sire fine white calves this season. Who will pay for this loss?" asked Sir Rummer.

"What payment do you require?" asked King Arthur.

Sir Rummer considered Arthur and Gawain before replying, "I want you, King of Britons, to undertake a quest. If you promise to discharge it, I will let you and all your party free from the Greenwood."86

---

85 And this is still not how it happens in the better known stories. The Earl is either trying to keep the story simple or connect with the Greenwood setting.
86 Although the Earl's concept of the Greenwood appears to be somewhat darker than his companions'.

And Gawain, young and foolish as ever, said, "Let me take on your quest, uncle! There is no enemy so great, no battle so bloody that it will hold me back from achieving it for you."

"You have another penance, puppy," said Sir Rummer.

"It will not be great enough to stop me completing whatever quest you set my uncle," said Gawain.

Sir Rummer laughed at the boy's impudence.

"Do you not want to hear what the quest is? Or what your penance is, puppy?" he asked.

But Arthur replied before Gawain, "Why would you release us all before I have completed the quest?"

Sir Rummer replied coldly, "Can I not trust the word of a king that he will return within a year and a day to give me the fruits of his quest or face the punishment that comes with failure?"

Arthur's hunting party muttered and whispered their distrust of the elfin knight amongst themselves but Gawain was too hot-tempered to pay attention.

"If there is any punishment for my failure on

my uncle's behalf, I will accept it," he said. "My uncle's word is set in stone and mine is carved beneath."

"Done," said Sir Rummer, just as Arthur said, "The boy knows not what he says."

"Your penance, puppy, is to marry my sister," said Sir Rummer. "Your quest, on behalf of your uncle, is to return to me in a year and a day to tell me what it is that women most desire."

A ripple of laughter went through the hunting party for no-one considered Gawain experienced enough to have the first clue about a woman's desires. And then they started shouting opinions, such as "money", and "land", and "children", and "love", and "sex", and "marriage". Sir Rummer ignored all of these.

"Well?" he asked.

Gawain looked at King Arthur and then back to the knight. "Will your sister accept the hand of a man about to begin questing?"

"Brave. Brave but foolish," said Sir Rummer with something resembling amusement. "If she likes you, she is as like to go with you as wait for you."

Gawain did not expect a woman to desire any

such thing but held his counsel. Instead, the boy asked, "And where am I to meet her to wed her?"

"There is a chapel on the edge of the woodland," said Sir Rummer. "Wait there as the party leave the Greenwood -- and return there in a year and a day with the answer to my riddle."

Gawain said, "So be it. I swear to complete this quest for my uncle, on my honour and on his. And I will marry your sister if that is my uncle's wish."

"It is your penance," said Sir Rummer.

"I have done no wrong that requires a penance," said Gawain. "I only protect my uncle and his honour."

"Then it is my wish that you undertake this or your uncle, you and these other hunters will remain trapped in the Greenwood forever," said Sir Rummer.

"It will be so, good knight, if our apologies are not enough," said King Arthur.

Sir Rummer strode away without answering.

"How will he know if we ignore his demands?" asked one among the hunting party.

"What matter if he does if we are gone from

the Greenwood before he realises?" asked another.

And the hunting party hurried from the cover of the trees. Except for Gawain, who stopped and waited by the chapel, just as Sir Rummer had ordered and as Gawain had promised. He waited as the sun fell and then as the night passed, his horse grazing in what had once been the graveyard of a lost village.87

His bride came with the dawn. Though dressed finely in velvets and silks, the lady was the twin of her brother -- tall, broad, and angular. The features that looked powerful on him looked loathly88 on her and Gawain, too young to have learnt self-control, stared at her.

"You are ungracious to stare so at the woman who holds your life in her hands," said the lady.

Her voice was as deep and rough as her brother's. Gawain winced at every word.

"Is there a priest here to marry us?" she asked. "Or have your manners scared him away?"89

---

87 The Earl is presumably seeing a similar origin for this chapel as the church he is currently in, telling the story. It also makes the place that little bit more uncanny and otherworldly.
88 See the beginning of the story.

Gawain gathered himself together. "There is no priest here, madam. There has not been in many a year."

"Then let us take our vows before the Christian God without the intervention of another. Our promises are as good with or without another's help," said the Lady.

So, Gawain swore his life to hers and she swore hers to his before the abandoned altar, just as Sir Rummer had ordered and Gawain had promised. But Gawain hoped to flee his bride as soon as the words were spoken, and he hurried from the chapel as soon as the words had finished echoing through the building.

He was somewhat perturbed to find that his bride hurried along beside him, matching stride for stride. In truth, she could have out-stridden him with very little effort, but she kept by his side as if they were a pair of horses in harness.

"I must leave you to go on a quest for my uncle," Gawain stammered when it was obvious that his lady was not going to let him go easily.

---

89 And the lady is apparently unaware that a lost village means an empty church.

The lady smiled. "You are my husband, and I must do everything I can to ensure that you complete this quest. I will ride with you."

"You have no horse," said Gawain, for she had walked into the clearing about the chapel though the hem of her clothes remained clean and unstained.

The lady smiled again and mounted Gawain's horse--who may have huffed at the load. Gawain had no choice but to walk, leading his mount.

The couple travelled the length and breadth of Arthur's kingdom and everywhere Gawain asked the people he met what it was that women truly desired. Many of the older knights and merchants[90] laughed and told him to ask his wife, who obviously had more experience of life. The younger men replied in much the same way that the hunting party had.

His lady, however, talked kindly to their wives, and their children, and their slaves, and their servants, and their vassals, and their priests.[91] Each place they left waved fondly after

---

90 At this point, it's clear that "everyone" means "men of particular status or income" to Gawain.
91 Sir Rummer's sister feels differently about the definition of "everyone".

her as if she had saved each of them from some peril or other.

The only thing that Gawain92, the young fool, noticed, was that the people seemed to love his wife more than he, despite her ugly looks -- that he managed to avoid each night by drinking himself into a stupor in whatever inn or hall they were being sheltered in.

When the year had almost past, Gawain brought his wife home to Carlisle.93 He shrank away from the laughter of his former companions and begged an audience with his uncle, leaving the lady to cope with the court's disdain on her own.

"Uncle," said Gawain as soon as he was before King Arthur. "I am failing in this quest of ours."

"Does no-one know what a woman truly desires, then?" asked Arthur.94

"No," said Gawain. "I am set to return to Sir Rummer with no answer and I must accept whatever

---

92 The Earl considers young Gawain to be an idiot. I agree.
93 Northern versions of Arthurian stories, particularly ones that favour Gawain as the hero, often consider Carlisle Arthur's capital.
94 And yet no-one even asks Guinevere, let alone any other woman.

punishment he gives. No doubt I will lose my head."

"Sir Rummer can hardly hunt you down if you do not return to the chapel. Even if he does, he has a whole company of knights and men-at-arms to get through before he can harm you," said Arthur.

Gawain stared at his uncle.95 "I am married to his sister."

"We can hold her in your chambers so that she cannot betray us to her brother," said Arthur.

And Gawain remembered how kind his lady had been to everyone they had met.

"No," said Gawain. "I shall go to my fate. I gave my word."

He turned and left his uncle, but he did not go to his wife, avoiding the gossip and laughter he could hear from the courtiers around her.

That night when the couple retired to Gawain's chambers, he asked, "What does a woman desire?"

The laughter he heard then was finally his wife's.

Gawain, chastened, slept across the door so

---

95 And this is how it feels to find out your heroes are flawed people.

that none might disturb his wife's sleep.

The second night in Carlisle, Gawain asked again, "What does a woman desire?"

His wife did not laugh that night. Instead, she replied with a question of her own. "Would it make you feel better to tell people that I was cursed with this loathsome form?"[96]

"You are not loathsome," said Gawain, remembering her kindness.

But Gawain slept across the door again, for he could not bring himself to share a bed with his wife no matter what her kindness.

On the third and final night in Carlisle, Gawain once more asked his wife, "What does a woman desire?"

To which his wife said, "If this were a curse with a silver lining, and I could be a beautiful young woman half the day, would you choose that I was beautiful when others could see me or when I was in your bed?"

---

[96] At this point, it's worth saying that the Earl's telling of this story is significantly different from the traditional versions. Although it seems to be heading to more or less the same place.

Gawain had no answer and his lady simply sighed.

"A woman desires to have her way in all things," she said. "If there was a curse then it would be broken by you telling me that the choice was mine."

And, again, he did not give her the opportunity to have her way with him.

The next day, Gawain left his chambers before his wife could wake and rode for the Greenwood alone. He found the chapel once more and waited while his horse grazed the lost graveyard again.

With sunset, Sir Rummer arrived.

"Well, boy," said the elf knight, "do you have an answer to my riddle?"

Gawain did not reply.

"Have you failed to find an answer?"

Gawain still did not reply.

"And here I thought all married men knew what their wives wanted? After a year of marriage, you should be a master of this knowledge!"

"I am sorry for my discourtesy when we met," Gawain with sincerity.

"Ah! Now you seek to escape the punishment

for not answering my riddle!"

"And I am sorry for the discourtesy I have shown you over the last year," said Gawain. "But I did not love you and it is better that I did not lie to you."

Sir Rummer stepped back as if he had been struck.[97]

"And now I realise that a woman truly desires the same as a man: to make her choices for herself," said Gawain.

Sir Rummer did not stop Gawain when he mounted his horse and rode away, so it is assumed that Gawain answered the riddle truly.

---

[97] This is not in the usual versions.

Chapter Nine: In which a great storm breaks

John Barleycorn looked at Dolly, and then Hugh, and then each of his yeomen. Each one gave a little nod or a little shake of their head.

"Are you saying this wife you say you have is loathly?" he asked the Earl.

"The more I know her, the fairer she seems," said the Earl. "But the more I see that others slight her and think her less womanly for the things I find beautiful."

Dolly smiled. "That's very romantic."

"It's insane. The lady is either beautiful or she isn't," said John Barleycorn.

"You will have to forgive our leader," said Taliesin. "He has little interest in the finer points of women."

"Nor should he, in such fair company," said the Earl, sketching a bow in the direction of Dolly.

Dolly laughed. "I am not his companion, I'm his daughter."

"I liked the way you told the tale." Said Hugh.

"Thank you," said the Earl.

"I thought at first you saw yourself Gawain with how you changed his character,"[98] Hugh continued, "but your heart was with Sir Rummer, wasn't it?"

"The knight has my sympathies," the Earl agreed.

John Barleycorn laughed. "The man was fool enough to dress as his own sister. How could you sympathise with a buffoon[99] like that?"

"There was no sister, only the elfin knight," said the Earl. "But enough of that. Have I won your service or your absence?"

"We're not leaving," said John Barleycorn eventually.

The Earl nodded.

"It isn't because of your story, you understand," said John Barleycorn. "It's simply because the wind has got up while you were talking, and I have no wish to go out into it."

---

[98] Possibly too much.
[99] Although considered archaic, the word buffoon probably isn't old enough to be in this environment as it only dates from the 1540s. But, then, it's being used by a character who wasn't recorded until about thirty years later.

"Of course," said the Earl.

The wind grew through the night, rattling loose tiles and shaking the Greenwood trees. Then there came a moment when the rattling tiles and shaking trees were not the only things to move under its strength.

"Is that... Is the wall moving up there?" asked a yeoman.

He pointed to the highest tip of the western end wall where it met the two sloping sides of the roof, beyond the fallen font. The movement was small but enough to be seen.

"Maybe we should leave," Hugh said.

But John Barleycorn replied, "If it can move the stone of the wall, what do you think it will be doing to the trees? Here where they are untended[100], the dead wood will be falling and the old stools[101]

---

[100] This land is, after all, an abandoned village and essentially wasteland in that it is not under agriculture or forestry.

[101] A stool, in this case, is the base of a tree that is coppiced. Trees are generally coppiced, i.e. cut back to the stool, on a cycle whose length depends on species and intended use.

will fall."

As if to make a point, a tile fell from the roof, somehow falling through a gap instead of being blown away. When it shattered on the stone flag floor, the yeomen stared at the hole left behind for a while.

"It is difficult to tell," said Hugh, "whether that hole is larger than one tile."

"Where would the rest have gone?" asked another yeoman.

No-one answered and the yeomen shifted back into the confined vestry, with its lower walls and tighter roof, despite the Earl's protests. Here, the yeomen felt enough at ease to lapse into something resembling sleep, although they all sat in alert positions.

The Earl did not sleep, and he paced or crouched the vestry, grim-faced.

Towards dawn, Dolly crept over to him and asked, "Do you have everything you need?"

> And stools that are left uncoppiced well beyond their intended cycle will not have the root mass to counterbalance their stems or trunks and anchor themselves against a strong wind.

The Earl's answer was a curt, "I'm fine. I brought rags with me."

"And the pain?" Dolly asked.

"The same as anyone else's," replied the Earl. "And no worse than I have taken in a tourney or on the battlefield."

Dolly shook her head. "You have gone paler than anyone else I've ever seen."

"I'm fine," said the Earl, although his current crouch was curled as tightly as his body would allow.

"You've really been on battlefields?" asked Dolly.

"Do you doubt I'm capable of it?" the Earl asked.

Dolly shook her head again. "Hardly. I just wondered how you coped with the pain when you were supposed to fight."

The Earl smiled. It was not a pleasant smile.

"Of course," said Dolly and she left the Earl alone.

The Earl left the church while the sky was the grey of a twilight darkened by low cloud, although there was no rain, and the ground was dry. He made his way through the Greenwood copse[102].

He paused several times by root balls that had been pulled from the ground. In some cases, the stems had fallen against those another stool and were being held at an angle. In a few others, the stool and stems had taken neighbours in their fall. There was one stool that had been ripped so viciously from the ground that it lay some distance from the crater left behind.

The Earl stared at this one for a while and then buried the soiled rags he carried in the crater left behind by the stool's flight.

"I must go back to the Isle of Ravens," the Earl said on returning to the church.

John Barleycorn asked, "Right now?"

"Yes," said the Earl. But, after a moment, he said, "No. I can't go back like this. I cannot go back to my wife dressed like this. Give me your clothes."

"And what am I supposed to wear?" asked John Barleycorn.

---

[102] A copse is specifically a woodland managed by coppicing -- or formerly managed by coppicing, in this instance.

"Something else," replied the Earl.

He did not wait to see if John Barleycorn would follow instructions but began to strip off the servant girl's clothes. He wound the shirt around itself and used it to bind his chest before turning to John Barleycorn.

"Clothes," the Earl snapped. "Now."

John Barleycorn did not strip -- but managed to remove enough equipment from among his men that the Earl was soon dressed as one of the yeomen.

"Well, at least I am dressed as a man," said the Earl.

"You're welcome," said John Barleycorn.

The Earl waved a hand dismissively. "Why would I thank you?"

"I'm your esquire, not your servant," said John Barleycorn. "If I am your companion then I am your equal, or close enough that I am not to be snapped at like some dog."

"Sword," the Earl said as if John Barleycorn had not spoken.

Dolly held out her own short sword in its scabbard.

"Thank you," the Earl said, bowing briefly

over her hands as he took the blade.

John Barleycorn muttered, "Just because she's a woman and some noble's bastard."

But the Earl had already left the church again and was marching along the King's Road in the direction of the Ravens' Isle.

"The idiot is going to get herself killed," said John Barleycorn.

"Himself," said Dolly.

John Barleycorn laughed but did not argue as the Greenwood yeomen hurried to catch up with their new master.

Where the King's Road should become the causeway to the Isle of Ravens, the Earl and the yeomen stopped, if only because there was no way to go forward. The Causeway was flooded.

The tide was up above the sandy North Sea beach and the mudflats of the River Abus but was still below the height of the embankments that should have protected the causeway. However, there was water of equal depth between the flood defences. It was possible to make out gaps in the bank on the riverward side of the causeway, three of them, between the King's Road and the Isle of Ravens, which was now an island.103

"How am I supposed to get back now?" the Earl asked.

"We don't?" suggested John Barleycorn.

"You don't understand," said the Earl. "She's alone. The place is built of wood. Who's to say how much was lost last night? The burghers could very well kill her if they believe the port is beyond repair."

Hugh said, "That would be a terrible end to the story."

"The embankment," said the Earl. "We can walk across on the top of the seaward embankment."

"Is that an order?" asked John Barleycorn.

---

103 Although the layout is unlikely to be the same as any iteration of Spurn, this is a fair match for how the sandbar-based peninsula seems to die. The last time the peninsula was cut off was around 1600, with Spurn's current incarnation reforming about fifty to seventy-five years later. The only reason this hasn't happened since is because coastal defences were put up in the 1850s. It has since been decided not to renew these defences and Spurn should be seeing some major shifts relatively soon.

It was.

Chapter Ten: In which no bridges are built

The Greenwood yeomen and their new master arrived at what had been the gate through the wooden fence about the Isle of Ravens. The fence was still there, though damp, resting on the top of thankfully intact embankments. However, the gate had gone, replaced by a soggy bank that was attempting to slip back into the town and bring the water with it. Guards were watching labourers shore it up with planks of wood and cleanly worked stones.

"Where did you get those materials?" the Earl asked, brows drawn together in a frown.

"What's it to you, archer?" one of the guards replied.

John Barleycorn said, "Are you blind? Do you see a bow and quiver on this one?"

"Peace, John," said the Earl, then he asked the guard, "Don't you recognise me?"

"Should I recognise a mudlark?"104 the guard

---

104 An eighteenth and nineteenth century word for someone who scavenges through river mud at low tide for items of value, particularly London. While an anachronistic use in the wrong

asked.

"Should you not recognise your lord?" the Earl countered. "I have only been gone three days."

"My lord, you say?" asked the guard.

His fellows stepped forward, no longer focussed on the labourers, their hands moving towards their sword hilts.

"Get someone who will recognise me and let me enter the town," said the Earl.

The guard smiled. "Enter the town and I shall arrest you for impersonating a noble."

Another guard muttered, "A noble wouldn't wear such poor leather armour or such common arms."[105]

"I'm not going back," said John Barleycorn. "I want a warm fire and an ale before I even think

---

geographic region, I think we can safely say the Earl and the yeomen are somewhat muddy from their walk along the bank along the flooded causeway.

[105] Although the clothing has not been particularly well described earlier, it's highly likely that it won't be particularly high class given that the original owners have been been living rough in the Greenwood. The sword has been described simply as a short one but, again, is probably of a rough quality.

about anything else."

"I'm not going back either," said the Earl.

"And I'm not staying on this God-forsaken slurry[106] all day," John Barleycorn continued.

Dolly snorted. "You won't have to. The sea is on its way out and it should be low tide in a few more hours. You'll be able to stand on another bit of mud soon enough."

"If you arrest us," the Earl began.

"Who is this 'us' you speak of?" asked John Barleycorn.

"If you arrest us," the Earl tried again, "Will you take us before the Countess?"

"When you are tried, perhaps, if the Countess thinks it worth her while," said the guard.

"Resist them," the Earl said to the yeomen, "but don't kill them or my wife will be upset."

And he stepped forward on to the pile of materials the labourers had already tried to shore up the gate-filling bank with. The labourers

---

[106] If it were really slurry (a semi-fluid mix of water and earth) they wouldn't have made it this far. However, it's probably not the safest place in the world to stand.

scattered as he drew his sword.

"Stupid as well as ugly," the guard said and drew his own.

He had less to say about being pummelled in the face with the short sword's hilt, instead of managing to block the undercutting blade as he had expected. He wobbled as he stepped back.

The yeomen drew their bows, pointing arrow heads at the guards.

"Hold them," the Earl said to John Barleycorn.

"As you wish, my lord," was the reply.

But the Earl did not stay to hear it as he hurried to his wife's palace.

At the palace, the Earl found the guards on duty too distracted by burghers clamouring for an audience with the Countess to notice him slip in through the servant's entrance.[107]

His own rooms were unguarded[108] and he

---

[107] I guess we can assume a certain snobbery applies to how badly the servant's entrance, previously unmentioned, is being watched.

[108] He did say he would be gone for a week. There's also a lot going on

changed his muddy yeoman's clothing for his own and armed himself with his own sword, although he strapped the small sword around him as well.109 Clothed once more as the Earl, he hurried to the hall, which rang with the chatter of more burghers venting frustrations. He ignored them and stared towards the throne110.

"My lady?" the Earl called.

The room fell silent, and everyone turned to look at him.

"Yes?" the lady on the throne replied.

The Earl snarled and grabbed her by her ear. "You are not the Countess. You should not be in such a hurry to steal her place, viper, else you might die of your own venom." He pushed the Mistress away from the throne. "Where is my wife?"

The Mistress clutched her swollen belly as

---

following the recent storm that probably required the Countess to use the guards elsewhere.
109 I assume so that he can return it to Dolly, not so he can dual-wield.
110 Thrones don't just belong to monarchs and popes. In this instance, it's the seat the Countess (or the Earl) would be expected to take while holding court -- i.e. hearing the burghers' problems and passing judgements on legal issues.

the burghers caught her and prevented her from falling. They muttered but no-one answered the Earl.

"Guards!" he called out. "Guards! To me!"

The burghers drew around the Mistress, who cried loudly about the injustice the Earl was doing. "You are not the <u>real</u> Earl, just a puppy who has wed his widow!"

"Get this... woman from my lady's house!" the Earl told the guards. "And someone tell me where my wife is!"

"The Countess is resting in her rooms," one of the burghers said. "She fled us with some excuse of a headache. Her lady-in-waiting has been kind enough to listen to our concerns in her stead."

"She has no right to do so," said the Earl.

"Then who will listen to us? You? You weren't here to do your duty when the storm came and you're too scared of your wife to do it when you're here, anyway," the burgher replied.

"Guards," the Earl said, "escort these gentlemen away with the Countess's former lady-in-waiting. Today's hearings are over. When you have done that, my esquire and his company are at the town gate needing entry."

The burghers protected the heavily pregnant Mistress as the group were herded form the palace by the guards. The Mistress herself panicked.

"My boys, the Earl's sons. I can't leave them!"

She tore at the men holding her back until one among them said, "We will send for your sons, my lady."[111]

"Don't bother," said the Earl. "I'll be sure to send them after you."[112]

The Mistress froze, causing the whole group to stall[113] outside the palace. She turned to look at the Earl.

"My sons will avenge the desecration of their father's memory," she swore. "They will correct the

---

[111] Given that, as the sons of the late Earl, the Countess's second husband, they may provide a suitable figure-head for a rebellion against the Countess, this is unlikely to be for altruistic reasons.
[112] Which, given the above, just goes to show how naive the Earl is with respect to keeping estates.
[113] Despite the association with engines since the early twentieth century, this word has actually been in use since the fifteenth century -- it's not as anachronistic as you'd think.

injustice you have caused today."114

"I look forward to it," said the Earl.

He left the crowd to disperse and go back to their own business as he expected. The burghers muttered as they withdrew. One of them offered his arm to the Mistress, mouthing pleasantries about how healthy she looked and how soon the baby was due.

Inside the palace, the Earl ran for his wife's rooms and pushed aside the blades of the guards at her door as if they were nothing more than grass.

"My lady," he said. "Are you well?"

She stood and turned to him. "Husband? But you were to be gone for a week?"

"The storm. It caused damage where I was and I had to come back," he said.

"Your bolt-hole was destroyed?" asked the Countess.

"I had to know how the storm had passed here," said the Earl. "I had to know that you were well."115

"As you can see, I am fine," she said.

---

114 See? Those boys are trouble.
115 Aawww!

"I have an esquire," said the Earl. "I found him in the Greenwood with a company of archers. And I have found you a lady-in-waiting to replace your late husband's Mistress. And--"

The Countess frowned. "Really? Is she another young and pretty thing? How many minutes did it take you to realise you desired her more than your wife? Or did you find her last time you ran away?"

"It's-- It's not like that," said the Earl. "I thought that you could use a woman you could trust."

"And you trust after, what? Three days? Less? More? Did she just have to look at you or did you manage to see her body before you came to your decision?"

"She is my esquire's daughter," said the Earl.

"Has that ever stopped a lord who decided to take a woman?" the Countess asked.

Chapter Eleven: In which a port is rebuilt

As soon as the waters of the Abus and the North Sea were low enough, the Earl returned to the place where the town gate had once been and oversaw the building up of the flood bank there. With no burghers' cases to hear, the Countess called upon the captains and merchants of the port to send for materials to repair the banks that had broken along the causeway and to build up the causeway itself so that it would always be above the highest tide.

The burghers, of course, returned in their own good time to complain about how houses had been torn down to provide the materials to fill the gateway. It didn't matter how many times the Countess pointed out that she had sacrificed dressed stone from internal palace walls as much as they had sacrificed wood and earth.

"Your maids told me that their Mistress's son is the true earl of Ravens' Isle[116]," Dolly said to

---

[116] A title which hasn't actually been used anywhere else in the story so is presumably just a coincidental combination of station (earl) and the place he would be expected to rule from

the Countess on her first evening. "They told me so before they realised I was to be your lady-in-waiting."

"Then I shall make sure the guards are seen about the palace," said the Countess.

She passed the instruction along to the Earl over breakfast, along with another. "We should have a child to ensure we can hold the port."

"In due course," the Earl replied and then said to John Barleycorn, "Ensure your yeomen are seen overseeing the labourers and helping with the rebuilding."

"What do good yeomen know of repairing structures?" asked John Barleycorn.

But the yeomen were all seen carrying drinking water and bread from the Countess's stores to those who laboured on the flood banks. And the Countess, distracted by the work, did not mention children again.

Over the days, the port recovered -- as the wooden houses by the old gate dried, as the causeway was built up with stone, as the river was dredged

---

(the Isle of Ravens).

for mud[117] to cover the newly strengthened embankments and replace the land stolen by the storm. A number of the floating piers had cosmetic damage from meeting a hull to closely, a number of hulls needed work from kissing a pier to passionately and were brought into the old stone quays where repair work was easier, the lock gates were stiff but had held.

"It was a great storm like I have never seen," many people were heard to say.

"It's like won't come again in our lifetime," became the standard response.

The Chaplain expressed opinions about Great Storms as a punishment for sin[118] at every

---

117 The river, whether you consider it the Humber Estuary or this fictionalised Abus, will be brackish at this point and the mud will be salty. But it will improve in quality with time given that it will also be rich in other nutrients. Although it's unlikely that anyone relies on these fields for their livelihoods and it's more likely that they are more a show of wealth and power.

118 Not an uncommon opinion, at least according to the papers associated with various monasteries. It should be noted that they're usually questioning the morals of someone who disagreed with

opportunity, particularly his regular services. The services were more heavily attended than usual, so full that it was apparent every household was at least represented in the House of God.

"Pfft," said Hugh, every time he was present to hear the opinion. "It is only show that there is or was something wrong in the world. Now that the Usurper is overthrown119, there will be no more storms."

"Not that old thing again?" John Barleycorn would say.

The looks that Hugh gave him were not happy.

"We have all got sins against our names in Heaven's ledger," the Earl said, on a couple of occasions.

To which John Barleycorn snorted, "Some more than others, I've no doubt."

And the Countess's maids ran to tell the Mistress of the comments.

"Why do you keep them?" Dolly asked.

The Countess replied, "Who else would I

---

them, however.
119 Not news that has otherwise been shared so presumably not considered relevant to this story.

employ? There is no-one who can be spared from the repair works."

"The works have become improvements," said Dolly. "The repairs were finished days ago."

"I must go," the Earl said over a breakfast almost four weeks after his return.

"You have only just come back," said the Countess. "The repair works--"

"Are as complete as they are likely to be. We have seen many high tides and held them out," said the Earl.

The Countess shook her head. "But there have been no storms. What if there is another great storm? You know what damage it did -- not just here but throughout England."[120]

"Then perhaps God wills that there be a

---

[120] If it was big enough to be a true Great Storm -- a strong European windstorm -- like the 1362 Grote Mandrenke, it's likely that significant damage was also seen in what we now consider the Netherlands, Germany and Denmark amongst others. These strong European windstorms happened quite often in the thirteenth and fourteenth centuries.

storm," said the Earl.

"You believe that as little as I," said the Countess -- and her maids exchanged a look. "Are you so poor a man, so craven that you must run from your wife and your duties?"

"I am not running. I will return within the week, just as I did before," said the Earl.

"My former husbands were not so weak that they left me in my time of need," said the Countess.

The Earl folded his hands in his lap and replied, "Your previous husbands were not inclined to doing their duty. After all, one of was a supporter of the Usurper and the other had a mistress who covets your title."

"The Usurper had not yet shown his true colours at that time," said the Countess. "And everyone will forget that whore's so-called rights when you provide me with an heir."

"You would have to share a bed for that," one of the maids muttered.

"They'd have to do a damn sight more than share a bed," said John Barleycorn loudly, "and it would take a miracle for anything but screams to result from that."

"Sir, guard your tongue," said the Earl.

The Countess stared at her husband's esquire. "Are you truly so impudent that you would say such a wicked thing while sat at my table?"

"How is it wicked?" asked John Barleycorn.

"Be quiet!" the Earl hissed.

"I am not so old as you, sir," the Countess said, "and I, at least, have manners fitting to noble company."

John Barleycorn laughed. "I am, I admit, likely the oldest person here. Save for Hugh."

"I don't believe that's the point my lady was trying to make," said Dolly.

"Then perhaps she should make her points more clearly," said John Barleycorn.

"You are an oaf," said Dolly.

"But I am at least as much the company's oaf as I can be," John Barleycorn replied.

"Misfortune has always dogged us," said Dolly.

"Enough, you two," said the Earl and they immediately fell silent.

The Countess stood. "And enough from you, puppy. My father always said that you can tell the quality of a man by the company he keeps. You keep ill company, and I was fooled into thinking more of you by how well your King seemed to think of you."

"Our King," said the Earl. "After all, have we not had news that the Usurper is gone since the storm?"121

"You are no man," said the Countess.

"I think she knows you already," said John Barleycorn.

"Now I realise you're nothing more than a man-at-arms or yeoman122 raised beyond his station because the King had a use for you123," said the Countess as if he had not spoken. "You are certainly not the man my father was."

"I have no idea what kind of man your father was," said the Earl.

"A great one," said the Countess. "He built this port124 and made our Estates famous throughout

---

121 Just as Hugh said earlier. And, no doubt, there are stories in this world about how the storm was a sign of the Usurper's sin and lack of fitness to rule.
122 She's saying he's too common.
123 She's returning to the implications from her telling of Blondel.
124 Presumably not literally. He probably

Europe."

"Tell me about him," said the Earl.

The Countess turned, as if to leave, then sighed and turned again. She sat down at the table and folded her hands just as the Earl had done earlier.

"I will tell you a story instead," she said.

---

watched the peasant-labourers building it while not talking to the peasant-but-not-as-poor-merchants that made use for it.

The Tale of Graelent, as told by the Countess

The Lay of Graelent is an anonymous Breton lay (or lai) probably composed in the late twelfth or early thirteenth century. It draws heavily on a lay by Marie de France (see the Earl's telling of Bisclavret) and has been attributed to her in some translations.

There was once a handsome Breton knight called Graelent who served the king of his day. This king was land-hungry and fought many wars against his neighbours -- and all of his loyal vassals brought their might to the joust, and the tourney, and the battlefield as their king demanded.

Graelent, from an old family as noble as the king's, won great honour in these feats. He became known as the handsomest, the wisest, the hardiest, the most valiant of the king's knights.125 Indeed, so well-known was he for being the flower of Breton

---

125 If the Countess is using Graelent as a parallel for her father, she's very proud of the late, apparently great Earl.

chivalry that the queen decided she would take him as her lover.126

The queen called for Graelent to come to her chambers but, though the knight attended her immediately, he turned away all her advances with words of simple courtesy and gentle wisdom. Reminded that they both owed loyalty to the king, the queen relented and allowed Graelent to leave without demanding that he return her feelings.

Graelent returned to his labours in the field for his king and the queen, without sight or sound of him, reconsidered his words to her. In time, her love turned bitter and curdled into a sour hatred. It overflowed into sharp words that ran into her husband's ear and set his heart against the faithful Graelent.

The king, so manipulated, withheld payment for the service given by Graelent and his followers, even to the point of begrudging any praise of the knight's prowess spoken in the king's presence. In a matter of weeks, the great knight's fortunes and birth right had been lost and his retinue dispersed,

---

126 A significantly more dangerous parallel to be making.

with only a horse to his name.

    Graelent was disheartened. He had been nothing but a faithful and loyal knight to his king, despite the temptations set before him. Even when he had realised that his ruin was coming, he had not left the king's service for another lord's because he could not break his oaths so easily. Yet, he could not believe the queen had been so petty as to turn the king against him[127] and could only wonder whether there was some slight or crime he had committed in the field.

    So Graelent mounted his horse and rode out into the countryside with no destination in mind, lost in thought, until he surprised a white hind[128] in a Greenwood thicket. The hind leapt and Graelent's horse leapt after it, the knight suddenly intent on the chase for white deer always render their hunter good fortune. But the knight was soon distracted again for the hind led him to a grassy

---

[127] The Countess seems to have a bit of bitterness here -- it's rarely mentioned whether Graelent knows how his fate came about.
[128] Some English translations insist on using the term "white hart" but still refer to the animal as "she".

clearing where three beautiful maidens bathed in a woodland pool.

Graelent stared at this scene, the hunt for good fortune forgotten. He noted that the three maidens had left their clothes hung from a certain bush, and that two young servant women tended a small camp away from the pool. But mostly he noted that the three bathing maidens were the most beautiful women he had ever seen, although one was comelier than the others.129

Without really knowing what he was doing, Graelent found himself by the bush that held up the maidens' clothes. As with their owners, the clothes were the finest he had he had ever seen but there was one set that was richer and more beautiful than the others. It was so much so that he couldn't help but reach out for the velvet130 mantle.

The two servant women noticed his movement and cried out, which caused the maidens to turn and notice the knight's presence.

---

129 It's more usual for there to be one maiden.
130 Velvet in Europe dates from around the fourteenth century. It was probably developed in East Asia.

"Hold, Graelent," the finest of the maidens called out. "Stealing my clothes will bring you no profit."

The words stayed Graelent's hand and stirred his pride. "I am no merchant nor pedlar to sell stolen cloth."

"Then release my clothes," said the lady said.

"You may have them," said Graelent, "if you come and take them."

"I do not know you to trust whether you will leave me unharmed," said the lady. "I think I may be safer here with my companions."

Graelent said, "I swear on God and His mother[131] that you will be safe from harm. I would never willingly cause you any hurt, now or ever, for you are the most beautiful part of creation I have ever seen."

Seeing that Graelent would not be moved, the lady stepped from the pool and approached the bush. Seeing more of her beauty, the knight fell to his knees.

---

[131] Which, given how little religion the Countess has shown, is somewhat unusual.

"My lady, I beg that you take pity on a poor knight and grant me a taste of your beauty."

The lady withdrew. "Graelent, you are too bold. My lineage is greater and more noble than yours, yet you treat me as if I was a common maid."

Graelent, not put off, begged that she show mercy, "For I no longer had a lord to serve, having nothing to give in service. So let me give my heart for your love and I shall serve you with a loyalty unmatched."

"I will grant mercy," said the lady, "if you return to your lord and never speak of me to anyone."

"And when I have returned to the king's service?" asked Graelent.

"Forget me," said the lady.

Graelent shook his head. "How can a man forget the sight, the sound, the taste, the feel of paradise once seen, and heard, and tasted, and touched?"[132]

The lady replied only with, "If you would keep me longer, then you must hold your tongue forever. I may stay with you day and night but if

---

[132] Apparently the smell goes unmentioned.

you talk of me to your companions, if I am seen, if they learn of my existence, I will leave."

"I swear," said Graelent, too dazzled by her beauty to say anything else.

She smiled. "Then you were worth the effort I took to hunt and capture you.133 Leave me and mine to regain our composure and I will send a servant tomorrow, to prepare for my arrival."

Graelent did as he was told and returned to the king's service. At first, he rode full of hope but, as night fell and the king's dislike settled around him once more, hope left Graelent and doubt plagued him with thoughts of five comely women laughing at his stupidity.

However, his embarrassment was relieved the next day when a mounted man in plain but fine clothes called by and begged leave to present himself as the loyal servant of Graelent's lady134.

"What word?" asked Graelent. "When does my lady arrive?"

But the servants only answer was that the fine grey horse he rode had been sent for Graelent

---

133 Which would explain how she knew his name.
134 Still apparently unnamed.

and he himself had been sent to serve the knight, to pay the wages of the knight's household and to generally take charge of the household.

Even though the servant had not brought the news Graelent would most liked to have heard, that of his lady's arrival, the knight was much heartened by the gifts. Indeed, while the servant dressed Graelent's lodgings as befitted a noble knight of substance, Graelent recalled all the men who had previously served under him and invited the friend-knights who had set him aside with the king's dislike to a great feast. Because the new manservant ensured that the household was rich and the feasting richer, Graelent shared his good fortune and in doing so returned into noble society once more.

His lady came soon after the first feast. Staying at his will and his pleasure, she laughed with him through the day and loved him through the night. Still, he was a great enough knight that he did not neglect society and he garnered much honour attending tournaments, although he did not raise his lance again for his king.

The king, seeing this, wondered at Graelent's new riches. The queen, hearing of this, wondered at what lover he could have taken when she had not been enough. Where the king only sought to ensure that some of those riches came to him, however, the queen's plots ran deeper.

At Pentecost, when it was the tradition for all the nobles who held land from the king to feast at the king's table, the queen whispered to the king, "I have heard that some among the knights--" she looked at Graelent "--say that I am too old and haggard to be called your queen."

The king, rightly proud of the prize he had in his queen, was outraged and bade her stand before the gathered nobility.

"My lords," he cried. "Is my queen not the most beautiful woman who ever lived? Have you ever seen a maid or lady more lovely?"

The queen was very fair and, whether it be politics or truth, all men at the feast complimented her on it. Except for Graelent who had the fortune to know a handful of women so beautiful they might be considered fair folk[135].

---

[135] Yes, that is the Countess punning as well as pointing out the otherworldly nature of Graelent's lady. This may have implications for her views on her

The queen cried out, "Sire! See how this knight dishonours me! See how he despises me!"

The king, enraged because an insult to his wife was an insult to him, demanded to know why Graelent behaved so badly.

"Sire," said Graelent as humbly as a worthy knight could. "Please, I beg you, do not treat your wife so ignobly and show her off like some pet. She is beautiful but one only needs to see something of the world to meet others as beautiful or more so."

"Oh? And have you met one?" asked the king.

Graelent simply said, "Yes."

"Really?" asked the queen. "Would this be the lover that no-one has seen?"[136]

So, the king had Graelent thrown into prison until such time as this beautiful woman appeared, though the knight begged for respite. He had, he realised, betrayed his lover as he had sworn not to and the fear of losing her drove him half mad.

---

mother.

[136] Which is an attempt at "if you don't like me you must be gay". Which, incidentally, was considered a much bigger sin than adultery, which would also technically be treachery if committed with the queen.

Word was sent to Graelent's household of his arrest, but the messenger returned saying that no-one could be found, and the rich fittings that had been there since Graelent returned from the Greenwood had gone with them. No-one the messenger had asked could tell him when the household had left or how.[137]

"As you cannot show this fair maid you boast so loudly of," said the king to Graelent, "you will be tried for your disloyalty and dishonour!"

So the king had the gathered nobles[138] discuss what punishment would suit Graelent's crimes best, although some among them had misgivings about accusing the knight of treachery as the king insisted.

As the debate began, a page disturbed the meeting to draw attention to the arrival of two young servant women mounted on fine palfreys.[139] The women were the most beautiful peasants the court had

---

[137] In the original lay, it is Graelent who is released to discover this.
[138] Presumably just the men -- as the queen is the only woman who has so far had a mention.
[139] Presumably the servants from by the pool on a pair of riding horses.

ever seen and easily a match for the queen. Although plain, their clothes were of better quality than anything in the king's household.

"Sire," said one of the women, "my lady bids you hold the sentencing until she has pleaded with you for her knight's deliverance."

The queen, hearing of these servants, hurried to see them and, once she had done so, was filled with jealousy. But the servant had asked so sweetly that the king agreed, despite his wife's anger. The queen had no choice but to run from the hall and take her shame with her.

Hardly had she done so when another page arrived with word of two more young women on even finer palfreys. These damsels[140] were so beautiful that the queen was forgotten, and the noblemen declared them angels.

"Sire," said one of the damsels, "my lady will soon be here to plead for her knight's deliverance."

And the king, aware that he had already met four women comelier than his wife, had Graelent

---

[140] Presumably the two other maidens from the pool.

brought to the hall to wait for the arrival of his lady.

The lady herself arrived shortly thereafter, mounted on a palfrey as fine as she, and silence fell on the gathering for there was not a man among them whose heart was not struck with jealousy by Graelent's good fortune. Graelent fell to his knees and begged forgiveness for breaking his promises to the lady even before she spoke, and she looked on him silently.

"Show mercy on a fool," he cried.

But the lady turned and left him on his knees in the king's hall.

"She is truly the most beautiful woman I have ever seen," said the king, and he had Graelent freed from his chains.

Graelent chased after his lady, waiting only long enough for his horse -- the grey that she had given him -- to be saddled before following her and her companions. But though he came as close as he had to the white hind, he could no more catch his quarry than he had before and his pleas remained calls rather than kisses.

In the Greenwood, the lady and her maids led

Graelent to a river that caused her to finally speak to him, when she realised that Graelent meant to follow them across.

"Do not attempt to cross the river," she warned him. "Though your horse is one of mine[141], it and you will be swept away should you try to cross. It will be the death of you."

But Graelent still followed and, as the lady had predicted, the river's current swept the grey horse from its feet and the knight was tossed aside into the water.

Seeing this, the four maids -- companions and servants both -- called out to their lady to save the man who had been her own fair lord for the last year. Their cries were so pitiful that the lady had no choice but to admit the love she still held in her heart, and she turned her own horse back to the river. With her own hands she caught Graelent and, as if some magic stopped the current that pulled on him, he was able to mount behind her.

So Graelent was saved and remained on the other side of the river in the Greenwood, until he

---

[141] Presumably a fairy horse rather than a normal one.

returned with his daughter142, though some say that he died in the waters instead.

---

142 This is a reference to another story where Graelent (as Gralon, or Gradlon) is a king of Brittany.

Chapter Twelve: In which a heart is broken

"I am not the man your father was, then," said the Earl.

The Countess replied, "Clearly."

When the Earl said no more, she added, "I know what use your king--"

"_Our_ king," said the Earl.

"What use _your_ king," said the Countess, "had for you and I will make sure everyone else realises it if you leave the Isle of Ravens again."

The Earl smiled. "You are mistaken in what you think you know."

"But probably not by much," muttered John Barleycorn.

The Countess stood again and walked away. At the door, she paused and said, "If you leave, do not bother to come back. I shall tell our people that you have died and seek a husband who has the stomach for producing the heir the Isle of Ravens needs."

"If that is what bothers you most about our marriage," said the Earl, "lie with any man you choose. The only requirement for inheritance is that you produce the child -- legitimacy comes when I claim and raise the child as my own."

The Countess left as John Barleycorn roared with laughter.

"Why not just tell her that it isn't your stomach that's the problem?" asked Dolly.

And John Barleycorn laughed again.

"Quiet," the Earl said to him, "or I shall send you to warm my lady's bed and father my children."

"Begging your pardon but I have no more stomach for that than she thinks you do," said John Barleycorn.

The Earl looked at Dolly.

Dolly shrugged and ran after the Countess.

"Are you not... together?" asked the Earl.

"Did not Hugh say as much when we met? I have known her since she was a child," said John Barleycorn. "She is my girl because I've raised her, and our affections do not go beyond that."

"Oh," said the Earl.

"But that doesn't matter,"[143] said John

---

[143] Not strictly true as alluded to in the notes with the Tale of Graelent. Sodomy was considered the kind of sin that doomed the whole community at the time

Barleycorn. "What matters is that my lord and his lady continue to hold what is theirs. At least while I'm in service to them. What good is a broken[144] master?"

The maids, unnoticed, exchanged a look and also left the hall. They did not follow their supposed mistress and her lady-in-waiting.

"Perhaps you should stay this time," suggested John Barleycorn.

"No," the Earl said.

"Dolly can help you--"

"No," the Earl said again.

"But--"

"No-one else can see me... like that," said the Earl. "And if Dolly is seen spending even a moment more than she needs to with me, the Countess and everyone else will assume I am like the last earl, preferring the maid over the lady."

"It would cool your wife's ardour, I

---

the lay was composed and the Church recommended excommunication--expulsion from the community--as the only way to save the other souls.

[144] Broken in the sense of insolvent has been in use since the sixteenth century at least.

suppose," said John Barleycorn.

When the Earl didn't respond, John Barleycorn added, "Some more, that is."

The Earl still did not say anything.

"Couldn't you at least bed her?" asked John Barleycorn. "It's not like you have to remove your clothes to please her."

The Earl stood and left the hall.

John Barleycorn stared at the remains of breakfast for a moment before deciding to finish them off.

The Earl did not follow his wife directly but, when it was time to retire for the night, he shooed Dolly and the maids from the Countess's chambers with little more than a look.

"You dare?" the Countess asked.

"Yes," the Earl said simply.

He stepped so close that there wasn't even a gap large enough for air between the two of them.

Then he said, "I will return in seven days, whether you see me or not. The King has commanded that I hold this port for him."

When the Countess would have turned from him,

he gently touched the soft skin of her wrist. He added in a whisper, "And it is time we gave your people a reason to believe your family will hold it forever."

"Why are you whispering?" the Countess asked.

"Because even Dolly won't be able to keep your maids from listening and taking their gossip to their Mistress," whispered the Earl, "and I would rather they did not know the truth -- that I cannot give you the children we need."

"An-- A jousting injury?" the Countess whispered.

"No."

"You just cannot perform the role of husband? Then what use are you to me?" the Countess whispered back.

"None," the Earl whispered, "but I was not left here because I was of use to you."

"Did you play the role of husband for the King or was he yours?" the Countess hissed.

"Neither."

"Then you merely pine for him and some other man plays the role when you leave the Isle of Ravens," the Countess whispered and she stepped away.

"I have never loved a man," the Earl said quietly. "Nor woman before you. I have only ever wished to be a knight."

"You have not loved me," the Countess said loudly.

"But I can," the Earl said just as loudly, "if you will let me."

The Countess said nothing.

The Earl whispered so quietly that she had to lean in to hear him, "And that would be enough to give your people hope of an heir for now."

"We could just pretend," the Countess whispered.

"I think your maids may be familiar enough with the deed to know when a woman is lying about her enjoyment," the Earl whispered back. "But if it is enough for you, then it will be enough for me. May it be enough for your former lady-in-waiting, too."

"Well, we are married," said the Countess, staring at her husband.

He smiled.

She smiled back.

The Countess had less to smile about in the morning when she woke to find the Earl gone, his sword hung on her bedchamber wall.

"Dolly! Dolly! Damn you, girl. Get this rubbish from my chambers."

She stared at it while Dolly hurried into the room.

"I take it back," said the Countess. "Do not take it from my chamber. Take it from my palace. Take it from my city. Take all of that good-for-nothing's things and throw them in the Abus at high tide."

Dolly said, "But when he comes back--"

"You can have the guards throw him in the river after them. But I doubt he will be that stupid," said the Countess.

"You didn't seem to think him stupid last night," said Dolly.

The Countess threw a pillow at her.

"If he returns," said the Countess, "I will tell everyone that he is a lover of men and incapable of fathering a child."

Dolly said, "Hadn't you better at least let

everyone think there may be a child until we've done something about that old Mistress of your last husband?"

"How dare he leave me like this!" the Countess screamed.

Dolly picked up the thrown pillow. "Well, that is a response that fits better with your night of... conversation."

"He's a puppy! A fool!" the Countess continued. "How can he... How can he love me like... and then leave me like that?"

"He has to be elsewhere," said Dolly.

"He has to be here," said the Countess. "He is the Earl." After a moment, the Countess added, "He is my husband."

"He has gone with the yeomen," said Dolly. "He will be back in several days."

"He is no longer welcome," said the Countess.

Dolly smiled. "Forgive me, my lady, but after last night, I doubt your honesty in this matter."

"I was tricked," said the Countess.

Dolly said nothing but helped the lady dress.

"I was seduced," said the Countess.

"By a lover of men who has no interest in

women," said Dolly with amusement. "Of course."

The Countess turned her back.

"I've been here a month. You think I don't know affection when I see it?" asked Dolly.

"Insolent wretch. Why did I agree to you as a lady-in-waiting? I've met dogs with better breeding."

"No doubt," said Dolly, "but you were desperate."

She ducked when the Countess turned to look at her but there was no lashing out to duck.

"He wishes to keep my estates for himself," said the Countess. "That's why he did it."

"He already has your estates, my lady. Land and title belong to whomever the King gives them to and the King has most definitely given you -- and your lands and your titles -- to that puppy of yours."

Chapter Thirteen: In which ravens fly

The Earl returned with the yeomen a week later, still dressed in his borrowed clothes. The guards at the gate spoke only to John Barleycorn.

"Why did they not acknowledge me?" the Earl wondered aloud.

"They just recognised me as the leader of my own men," said John Barleycorn. "Maybe they thought it was better to ignore you when you weren't in your proper state."

The Earl gave him a foul look.

"Or maybe they noticed your scowl and thought you were better left alone," John Barleycorn said.

"I grow tired of your company," said the Earl. "Perhaps you and yours should find somewhere else to be. Somewhere you can practice breathing through your nose, or chewing quietly, or some other survival skill."

John Barleycorn laughed. "I have lived long enough without knowing them. It seems a waste to put the effort in now."

But the yeomen dispersed into the port while the Earl made his way to the palace -- and found his path blocked by two guards with their polearms crossed.

"You have no business here, yeoman," one of them said.

A gust of wind blew as the Earl opened his mouth to speak, enough to make all three men wobble a little in their balance.

"Why can I not enter my own home?" asked the Earl, when the gust had passed.

The guard who had spoken before spoke again. "The Countess will not see you."

"She doesn't have to see me ever again," said the Earl. "However, I am the King's man, and the King has put me here. This is my home."

The wind gusted again.

"The wind's pretty strong," the guard who hadn't spoken yet said to the other. "Think we'll be in for a storm tonight."

"Straight down the Abus[145]," said the first guard. "It'll be something and nothing."

"Let me in," said the Earl.

The first guard said, "The Countess has ordered that you be thrown out of the port on sight.

---

[145] Essentially a westerly wind.

But none of us want anything to do with your sort. You're not wanted here by anyone. You might as well go."

"What 'sort' would that be?" asked the Earl.

The guards exchanged a look.

"I always knew there was something wrong about you," said the first guard. "I always knew you were watching us too closely. Well, we don't want your filth around here."

"If you scared that I liked what I saw, you can stop worrying about it," said the Earl.

The guard snarled but the Earl's sword, his borrowed yeoman's sword, was resting on the inside of the guard's thigh already.

"I have the measure," said the Earl, "and I watched you for mistakes like this. You are all half-trained and lazy. My yeomen and I could take this town within the hour."

The second guard stepped in, but the Earl quickly stepped clear of both of them, out of range of hands and pole-arms in a handful of steps.

"Unfortunately, I'm supposed to keep this place in one piece," said the Earl.

The Earl stood on the embankment overlooking the quays and piers. He watched the movement of the porters and sailors and captains and merchants. Late afternoon and the gusting wind had not slowed them.

"They're all moving so hurriedly but none of them seem to be getting anywhere," he said when John Barleycorn came to stand beside him.

"All over the port, they say you love men too much," said John Barleycorn.

The Earl smiled. "They appear to have confused us."

"My men and I are welcome to stay as long as we acknowledge the guard's captain as ours," said John Barleycorn.

"I'm a little surprised the sailors haven't made more of the opportunity," the Earl said. "After all, they have a reputation for wide ranging tastes."

"The town guards are a half-arsed excuse for a company of men," said John Barleycorn.

The Earl said nothing.

John Barleycorn added, "They'd be useless on a battlefield."

The Earl shrugged. "Battlefields are rare,

anyway. Any general with any sense prefers the siege. Well, to be on the outside of a siege."

"Aye," said John Barleycorn. "I suppose they're good enough for guarding a damp island."

"What time is high tide due?" asked the Earl.

"In the night," said John Barleycorn. "I think."

The Earl squinted towards the sky in the west where the grey of clouds hid the lowering sun.

"The wind has changed. When we arrived, it was from up river, now it's from the mainland[146]," the Earl said. "Nothing's been strong enough to blow anyone off their feet, but it's been getting up."

"You think a storm is coming?" asked John Barleycorn.

"I think the sailors and merchants are getting their cargo loaded so they can take the larger ships out into the river instead of having them run into the pier this time," said the Earl.

"Or maybe they're just preparing to leave with the tide."

"Well, neither of us know much about the sea," said the Earl. "We could both be wrong. Or

---

[146] Northwesterly.

even both right."

"Aye," said John Barleycorn.

Neither of them stopped one of the hurrying porters or sailors or captains or merchants to ask.

"The water looks a bit higher than I would have expected," said the Earl.

And still neither of them moved.

Before the sun met the land to the west, although still hidden behind fast-moving grey clouds, the ravens[147] took flight and rode the winds south.

"Grimsby's that way, right?" John Barleycorn asked.

"Land is that way," said the Earl. "Tell the merchants to make room on their ships for their families and neighbours."

"Land is closer to the north, surely?" asked John Barleycorn.

---

[147] Based on the legends around the Tower Ravens, this can be considered a Bad Sign. It's debatable whether actual ravens would be likely to behave this way. As stated before, it's improbable there were any ravens on the island in the first place.

The Earl said, "The wind might be too strong for them to fly against. And get a ship for the yeomen and the Countess's household."

"Just one?" asked John Barleycorn.

"At least one."

The Earl himself grabbed the arm of a passing merchant.

"What do you think you're doing, peasant!" the merchant said, trying to pull his arm away.

The Earl did not release him. "The river[148] is at the high-water mark already. It can only get higher if high tide isn't due until after dark. Get as many as your people to your boats while you can."

And the merchant[149] looked about at the river.

"The flood defences will be enough," he said.

"Now," said the Earl. "We stand a better chance in things built to float than we do in buildings that are not. The fleet is big enough to hold us all."

---

[148] The Abus, like any other estuary, will be tidal.
[149] Who was presumably familiar enough with the river to have already seen this and therefore not need telling.

The merchant spat on him. "Your kind is not welcome on any ship of mine."

"I'll bear that in mind," said the Earl.

But he released the merchant, who hurried off, and walked back towards the palace.

"I will send Dolly even if I can't get anyone else to listen to me," he called back to John Barleycorn.

The Earl broke into a run when the ground under his feet was stone quay instead of soil embankment. He paid no attention to those who refused to move out of his way and was past the guards before they had even had chance to register his presence.

"Dolly? My lady?"

He hammered on the door to the Countess's chambers.

"She will not see you," Dolly said through the door.

"She doesn't have to see me," said the Earl. "She needs to leave here. There is a storm coming and the water is already high."

"The defences will hold. The Island will hold," the Countess called loudly.

The Earl swore. "I would rather you floated than sank if it did not."

The Countess said something that could not be heard through the door and Dolly said, "We'll be fine."

"There is a ship in the dock," said the Earl. "John Barleycorn is arranging it. Please, go join the yeomen and be safe."

Although Dolly and the Countess talked, the words could not be heard on the Earl's side of the door. Even when the door was opened by the maids, just wide enough for them to slip through, the Earl could not make out the discussion. Instead, he watched the maids hurry away.

"Your maids have fled to their true Mistress," he called out. "Your former lady-in-waiting will be safely stowed in minutes."

"Let them go," the Countess shouted loudly enough for him to hear. "Let them all go. But I shall trust in my father's work."

"Your father was not planning for a tide as high as this one," the Earl said quietly.

There was silence behind the door and then it opened on Dolly loaded with a pack. "I am going to find John Barleycorn. I will have him wait for as long as the ship's captain will allow."

The Earl offered to carry the pack.

"Stay with your wife a little longer," said Dolly. "Perhaps you can talk sense into her."

"Why is everyone assuming that a puppy who has barely seen the sea more than once know anything about a coming storm?" the Countess asked.

The Earl looked to her -- and stepped back when he realised that she was bathing in front of the fire.

"My lady, forgive me for interrupting you but we must go," he said.

"We must wait," the Countess said.

Chapter Fourteen: In which the King returns

The King came again to the Countess's lands almost three weeks to the day after the storm[150]. The royal party arrived by the King's road rather than under sail and came to an abrupt halt at the ragged settlement that now marked where the road met the Isle of Raven's causeway.

"I had heard the storm's loss was beyond great," the King said, "but I did not realise whole cities were swallowed."

The island and its causeway were gone, with only some fragile-looking stone walls marking the location of the Countess's palace and the quays built by her father.

"Really?" a peasant woman marked caustically. "Did the new richness of Wyke[151] not give it away?"

---

[150] As mentioned in the notes for Chapter Ten, it's highly likely that the damage is far worse in the Low Countries (i.e. the Netherlands), what we now consider Germany, and Denmark. Coincidentally, the aforementioned Grote Mandrenke of 1362 was probably the final nail in Ravenser Odd's coffin.

[151] The pre-1293 name of Kingston-upon-Hull, which did see a slight expansion

"Who is in charge here? Where is the Countess?" the King demanded.

"Drowned in the Great Storm's tide, and good riddance," the woman sniffed as she picked up her work and scurried for the shelter of a rough hovel.

"And my loyal knight? Her husband, the Earl?" the King asked.

No-one answered.

"Who is in charge here?" the king demanded again. "Let them come to me."

But no-one came to bow the knee to the King, and no-one called out a welcome to the party.

"Find me the leader of this village, men," the King ordered.

The men-at-arms and knights who made up the party pulled apart the poorly built structures of the settlement, not even ceasing in their work when they pulled apart the mean building that served as a chapel for the former Chaplain of the Isle of Ravens.

"Brothers, why do you treat poor refugees

---

of its port business as Ravenser Odd failed and the merchants moved on to somewhere less prone to being swept away by a high tide.

from misfortune so badly?" the chaplain asked.

"Chaplain, I 'member you and your service," said the King. "What happened to you? Why are you here so? Why did you not return to the abbey?"

"Where else would I be but tending the flock the abbot gave me, sire?" the Chaplain asked.

"And do they respond to your tenderness?" the King replied.

The Chaplain sighed. "As well as ever."

"Who is the leader of this poor village?" the King asked. "Are you responsible for this, as well?"

"No, sire," said the Chaplain.

A knight, losing patience asked, "Then who is, Chaplain?"

But his companions, the other knights and men-at-arms, had disturbed the relative peace of the tiny settlement by pulling apart the walls that sheltered the Mistress as she gave birth, tended by the two maids who had once served the Countess.

"Sire, please!" the Chaplain said. "Tell your men to stop this mistreatment of men and women who have already suffered so much."

The maids and the Mistress screamed, although the disturbance did not stop nature taking its course. The men swiftly withdrew.

"Who is that? Her face is familiar," said the King.

"The late Earl's Mistress," said the Chaplain, "who was forced to serve as the wicked Countess's lady-in-waiting."

"Ah, yes. I remember that lady, now," said the King. "The pairing was not advantageous and yet the fool insisted on keeping her."

The Chaplain said, "At least she was faithful and not forced to marry a man she was barely acquainted with to cover her sin."[152]

The King laughed. "I'm sure that I would remember such sin."

The Chaplain frowned.

"The Countess, this wicked woman of yours, where is she now? Did she survive the storm?" asked the King.

"She is not mine," said the Chaplain. "And she has not been seen. We assume that she drowned

---

[152] Given that he was there for the hurried ceremony, it's unlikely the Chaplain actually believes this. However, it may be politic for him to remember it differently.

with that red knight[153] of hers."

"A red knight? I remember no red knight," said the King.

The Chaplain replied, "Sire, the knight you thought so noble and loyal hid his evil until you left. Then his unnatural tastes brought the wrath of God upon the whole port."[154]

"I have known the knight for several years," said the King. "This is the first time his tastes, as you say, have destroyed so many lives in England. And did God require that the people of the Low Countries pay for this 'sin' as well?"[155]

The Chaplain said nothing but frowned more deeply.

"I am come because the Great Tide[156] did much

---

[153] This is not a literal description. Nor does it relate to the modern concept of socialism. The Chaplain is just calling the Earl evil as well.
[154] It isn't uncommon for natural disasters to be blamed on immorality, even these days.
[155] The King is not amused.
[156] There is no storm event recorded with this name. This particular event seems to be a European windstorm causing with an exceptional storm surge (an area of low pressure, in this case over the North Sea) coinciding with a high tide.

damage to my kingdom, from north to south," said the King. "Although I am saddened by the Isle's loss, which I should have guessed by the return of your ravens to London157, I must make my Progress158 round all the wounded lands."

"Of course, Sire," the Chaplain said.

The King asked softly, "What happened to the Isle in the Great Tide? How were my friend and his wife lost to us?"

But a final scream from the Mistress's shelter interrupted the Chaplain's reply -- this one the cry of a baby, furious at being forced into the world.

"A girl!" cried one of the maids, running out

Something similar has happened on a rather large number of occasions.
157 Just in case we were wondering what happened to the birds the island was apparently named after.
158 A Royal Progress is a tour of major towns and cities, often done to remind the locals of the monarch's power and influence. This progress will presumably be a reminder that this King is the recent victor of a power struggle and that the recent storm was not caused by his own lack of morality, no matter how he disapproves of the Earl being called the cause.

into the open almost as soon as the cry had begun, "The Earl has a daughter, a little sister for his three fine sons!"

The King asked, "So the Countess's second husband had three sons by this mistress before he died?"

The maid curtseyed, "Yes, Sire," pausing briefly before running through the small settlement to spread the news further.

"A shame he could not get one on his own wife," the King muttered.

"She was unable to bare children with her first husband, either"159 the Chaplain said.

The King frowned at him. "I think it more his preference for his love, given that the marriage only lasted, what? Five years160 from wedding to funeral?"

"Many women bare children in five years of marriage," said the Chaplain.

---

159 In other words, it is the Countess whose femininity should be questioned, not her second husband's virility.
160 Hawise of Aumale's second marriage did, indeed, last five years. Although she gave her second husband, William de Forz, a son, also called William de Forz.

"Not if their men bed another instead," said the King. "He was a good knight but a poor husband."

"Do not dare!" a tired voice snapped. "Do not dare to talk of the late earl so!"

Another woman's voice whispered something, and the tired voice snapped again, "I do not care if he's the Pope or Jesus born again himself! How dare he doubt the honour of my children's father!"

The people of the village, the remnants of the Isle of Ravens, had gathered now, talking of their Mistress's labours and the late earl's posthumous daughter. The King surveyed them and then the entourage he travelled with.

"Have the merchants left this place entirely?" the King asked the Chaplain.

"No!" the Mistress snapped out and she pushed herself from her hovel, clutching the squalling newborn to her bared breast. "No. They are still loyal to the late earl, and they will not abandon us in our need. They have my sons already in Wyke and only seek suitable residence for me and my baby."

"Truly," the King said to the Chaplain, "You must tell me what happened here."

But it was the Mistress who replied, and she

replied with a story.

The Tale of Ys, as told by the Mistress

"Ys or Ker-Is (city of Ys), is a Breton tradition closely linked to very similar Cornish and Welsh tales. The tale as it is most known probably originated in the late fifteenth or early sixteenth century, putting it quite late in the anachronistic muddle of our framing story."

There was once a great city on the coast of Breton Cornwall[161]. This city was known as Ys and it was said to be a second Camelot and the true capital of that kingdom[162].

The grand stone docks and quays had been built at great expense with the stone carefully carried from quarries in-land. They sheltered a fleet unmatched in Christendom and many thousands of hearths were taxed within the city's walls. There

---

[161] Cornouaille -- probably named after the British Cornwall.
[162] This could be Cornouaille, Brittany or France, depending on what era is being described.

were rich green fields rolling down to the embankments and locked gates that held the high tides from the city.163

Ys was the beating, working heart of the kingdom, built by King Gralon164 to be the home of himself and his daughter, the princess Dahut, so that they might be closer to the sea than the true capital allowed. Indeed, the first building raised was said to be their great palace, another expensive transportation of stone arranged to face the sea.

Both Gralon and Dahut loved the sea. The first for the sake of his lost queen who had died before they made shore in Brittany, the second because it called to her in her dreams as if it were in her blood.165 That was the root of the city's downfall.

Gralon was a good Christian166 and the city

---

163 The Mistress is nothing if not obvious in her parallels.
164 See the Tale of Graelent.
165 A suggestion that Dahut and therefore the Countess is not fully noble or even human and that there is something very wrong with her.
166 Typically, the story of Ys is set at a time when Christianity is being adopted. However, the Mistress is telling it slightly differently. This

had developed into a place of beauty and virtue under his reign. However, as his daughter grew, it became obvious that her heart was black with pagan beliefs and witchcraft[167], and her influence brought the city and its inhabitants into disrepute.

Dahut would swim naked in the sea around the walls of the city each morning and evening. She presided over ceremonies on the beaches that sacrificed animals and even children to old demons. She tarried with anyone, man or woman, she took a liking to -- and had those who turned her down punished with public whippings so that the blood ran down their naked forms into the ocean waves as they screamed.

The bishop[168] and aldermen[169] of the city begged Gralon to control his daughter or to marry her to a man who could, but Gralon was besotted and

---

difference is surprising considering she didn't seem any more devout than the rest of the characters.
[167] A dangerous accusation, considering that belief in witchcraft was more heretical than being one for large chunks of the medieval era(s).
[168] Traditionally, this person is named as St Winwaloe.
[169] The Mistress presumably means city officials.

would hear none of it. Dahut merely laughed at them and offered her body to each of them.

Before her father, each of the men was virtuous enough to refuse her advances but, that night, Dahut was seen swimming with one of them. She was seen, before her swim the next morning, watching her servants throw something large and unwieldy into the sea before her. The alderman who had been seen with her the night before was not seen again.

"Sire," said the bishop, "You cannot allow this to continue.

He begged Gralon, again, to control his daughter, to punish her, to send her away, to find her a husband who might put an end to her lustful activities.

Gralon, again, refused.

"She will bring the wrath of God upon us," the bishop warned.

But Gralon would not listen.

The remaining aldermen decided to take matters into their own hands and visited Dahut in an effort to encourage better behaviour -- to at least hide her evil heart under a civilised, Christian veneer. Dahut laughed at them, and teased them, but followed the basic niceties of hospitality so that the aldermen were lulled into a false sense of security.

By evening, she had made drunken fools of them, turning the quiet audience they had begged for into an orgy170 that left them drained, stupefied and incapable of thought the next morning.171 They were fortunate, for they were all able to return to their wives and children172 as Dahut took her morning swim. However, each of them was unable to resist Dahut's exhortations to worship demonss and attend her secret rites. They lost all interest in their daily responsibilities and acted as if they were bewitched.

The wives of these aldermen came before Gralon and begged that he do something about his daughter's behaviour. But, again, Gralon refused to

---

170 Orgies were originally secret rites, which is exactly what the Greek and Latin meant. They didn't necessarily involve sex, just pursuing a state of ecstasy. Given the context, however, the Mistress is of the opinion that these things do involve sex.
171 Also, not a lot of love lost on these aldermen.
172 And that would be why.

listen.

"My daughter is the image of her mother," he said, "and her mother was the truest, most devout heart anyone has ever known."

The women went to the bishop who said, "The princess's sin will destroy us all.[173] Go home and pray for your souls."

The women did as they were told and their voices could be heard ringing through the many churches and chapels of the city, raised in prayer and praise to God. That congregation only grew as more people -- youths and maids and men old enough to know better -- were seduced to Dahut's worship and their families mourned, and prayed, and begged for the debauchery to end. The church bells rang at all hours, pealing the worship of God when voices grew too hoarse, and bodies grew too tired.

But Dahut only laughed.

She laughed until a red knight[174] arrived.

---

[173] There were (or are, if you are so inclined) great sins that ruined the souls of the community, not just the individual committing them. These are usually filed under "sodomy".

[174] In this instance, we can assume the colour is a Bad Sign about the knight's character. He may even be the Devil

Though no-one saw his face, the princess acted as if the most beautiful combination of features had been revealed to her when the knight said his good days.

"My lord!" she called to him.

The knight did not respond. Indeed, he acted as if he could hear nothing.

"My lord!" Dahut called again and sent one of her younger followers to intercept him.

Yet again, the red knight did not respond to her voice, and nor did he seem to notice the presence of the follower.

Dahut herself chased after him then, calling to him until she could place her hand upon the armour that covered his leg.175

"My lord," she said again when the red knight turned his helm towards her.

"My lady," he said. "Forgive me. I can barely hear anything over the ghoulish laments of the towns people. I had no idea that you were trying to attract my attention."

"I would silence them," said Dahut.

"I would that you silenced them, too," the

---

himself.
175 Forward and unseemly behaviour.

knight returned.

"I wish that the sea would rush in and take them all," said Dahut, "and I would swim at peace with the waves for eternity."

The red knight laughed.

"Tell me," Said Dahut. "Tell me what you wish. Tell me what I can give you."

She turned about and twirled her hair and did her best to draw a flattering answer from the red knight. He did not disappoint.

"Your body," he said.

But the night had barely begun when he began to lose interest and he was ready to leave both Ys and Dahut's bed. She held him and begged him to stay, ignoring the frown that came to his face just as she ignored the storm clouds that were beginning to gather on the horizon.

"Let me go," the red knight said.[176]

Dahut, in her devotion of this stranger, found herself telling him of how the sea-gates were

---

[176] This is not quite as the story usually goes but, given the Earl's rather public determination to leave the Isle of Ravens on a regular basis, fits the parallel the Mistress intends well enough.

locked and of how only her father held the key.

"I will give you this key," she promised, "if you come back to me."

The red knight laughed at her. "Take the key and open the gates. Let the sea roll in and take the pious fools who think their prayers will help. Spend your eternity in the sea's embrace."

In her hurt, and rage, and debauchery, Dahut took it into her head that this was the only way to win her red knight back to her side. So, while Gralon slept, his daughter crept into his rooms and searched for the key.

She found it on a chain around his neck, but even looking at it was enough to rouse, or partly so, the sleeping king.

"My love," he quavered, mistaking his daughter for the long-dead wife she resembled.

Dahut, for whatever reason, chose to humour him.

"Yes, my king?" she replied.

Gralon, unaware of his sin, reached for the memory of his queen. Dahut, uncaring of her sin as she always had been, submitted for the sake of the key around his neck.177

In the time it took her to lull Gralon back to sleep and steal the key, the storm broke against Ys's embankments. Dahut, perhaps driven mad by her latest sin or maybe just driven mad by her desire for the red knight who must already have been long gone from her bed, remained determined to open the sea-gates. She struggled to the first of the three gates.

At the very same time, the bishop was woken as if from a nightmare. He sat bolt upright in his bed, screaming in terror. In a matter of heartbeats, the man was running from his palace to the king's.

"Sire! Sire! We must leave!" the bishop yelled all the way there.

He refused to take "no" for an answer from the king's guards[178] and ran into Gralon's chambers.

"My king," said the bishop. "God is sending his fury this very minute. We must leave this city -- like Lot and his family[179] -- or be destroyed."

---

[177] Well, the Countess is very fond of her father's memory. Just not this fond, however.
[178] There is no comment on how Dahut got passed them.
[179] Running away from the destruction of Sodom and Gomorrah. Incidentally, Lot's wife had to stop and look back, leaving

Gralon roused and ordered that the alarm bells be rung. Unfortunately, the pious people of his city were already ringing the church bells and praying and singing to God. Many of them did not hear the alarm for their prayers. Those who were resting, as the bishop had been, were too used to the sounds of their city's piety to be disturbed by the added noise. So Gralon, the bishop and those disturbed by their night-time activities were the only people to be aware of the storm and the arrival of God's wrath. Those who had horses mounted and the ragged, panicked company charged from the city -- just as Dahut succeeded in opening the third sea-gate.

The sea broke over the royal palace like a wall collapsing. The water flooded through the streets of Ys, crushing the poorer houses in the first movement and destroying the others with the waves that followed.

Those who tried to escape on foot were dragged back into the water, as if the sea were animated by the demons their princess had been

---

Lot unattended with two daughters who apparently decided to seduce him or vice versa.

praying to. Their cries were drowned out by the roar of the waves and the church bells that still rang, accompanied by what was now the screams of the faithful.

The horses panicked and did their best to flee the thundering waves but few were fleet enough of foot. Only two horses escaped -- although their legs were soaked with salt-water before they did -- and these were the mounts of Gralon and the bishop.

And that was the end of Ys, perhaps the greatest city Christendom ever saw excepting Arthur's Camelot.

It is said that King Gralon lived the rest of his life at the true capital, Quimper[180], where he raised a church in the name of his faithful bishop when the good man died.[181] Dahut was never seen again but Breton sailors tell of a woman's laughter in the bay where Ys once stood when storms land there. Of Ys itself, there are those that say the most pious can hear the bells and praying of its lost people.

---

[180] The capital of both Cornouialle and Brittany.
[181] There isn't a church dedicated to St Winwaloe in Quimper.

Chapter Fifteen: In which the Mistress is rewarded

"The Earl you left behind had no interest in the Countess until she threatened to tell us the truth about him," said the Chaplain.

The maids nodded along.

"And then," one said, "he seduced her into his debauchery, knowing that no child would be conceived."[182]

"What exactly do you mean by this, Chaplain?" the King asked. "And you, women, what do you mean to say?"

The Chaplain and the maids flushed and were unable to get the words out. Until a maid finally managed to force words out.

"Everyone knew that he preferred another, Sire. Everyone knew that his heart was yours. And though we heard him please the Countess, we know he took no pleasure in it himself."[183]

---

[182] They either overheard discussions or, within about a month, decided that no child could be conceived, either because the Earl is incapable of making a woman pregnant (true) or because they know the Countess is incapable of conceiving (unknown).

"I never had hold of that good knight's heart," said the King. "Nor he of mine, for I have my own love."184

"Of course not, Sire," the Chaplain said.

The maids exchanged looks behind their silent Mistress and did not reply.

"I left a knight who could defend the port," said the King.

The Chaplain said, "Against everything but acts of God, and those he no doubt brought upon us for his debauchery."

"So, you mean God must wipe this much from the Eastern coast for the sake of one man's sin?" asked the King.

The Chaplain bowed his head. "Such sin condemns a whole community."

"You have condemned many communities," said the King.

"What does it matter?" asked the Mistress, "If both he and the Countess have been lost? We are the ones who survived. We are the ones who must rebuild or start our lives anew somewhere else when

---

183 Well, someone has to clean the sheets.
184 Who could be anyone.

we have lost everything and have nothing to pay for it with."

"Your three fine sons, madam. Where are they now?" the King asked.

"They shelter with us here," said the Mistress, still holding their suckling sister. "Though they may be out practising their archery."[185]

"Send for them. I would see how closely they resemble the second husband and earl," the King said.

The Mistress sent her maids running to find the children, evidently not among the hovels already partially destroyed by the King's party.

"He was my choice for the Countess, as well," said the King. "A great knight and a nobleman himself. I assume no-one has cast doubt on his interests or the goodness of his soul?"[186]

"Of course not," said the Mistress.

"No, Sire," said the Chaplain.

The King said, "If your sons are definitely

---

[185] Or running riot in the local countryside as unattended young children might.
[186] Adultery was considered a lesser sin than sodomy.

his, then they have some claim on his own barony."

And the Mistress dropped into a curtsey for the first time.

"Sire, you are too generous," she said, through gritted teeth.

"You expect more from me than this kindness?" asked the King. "His or not, they were born out of wedlock. They have no rights unless I make it so. Or did your late lover recognise them?"

"He recognised them and had them baptised as his children in the chapel," the Mistress said swiftly, casting a hurried glance at the Chaplain.

"Is this true? Did the late earl claim three sons?" the King asked the Chaplain.

"The chapel books have been lost in the flood, Sire," said the Chaplain not looking at either the Mistress of the King.

"But you no doubt held the service, Chaplain," the King said.

The Chaplain struggled to answer for a while before forcing out, "Yes, Sire. I baptised the three boys as the late earl's sons."

The King nodded.

The Mistress sighed and whispered something

quietly to her daughter.

The maids returned with three boys, muddied, and torn from their adventures, ranging in age from one old enough to serve as a page[187] to a youngling who barely came to a man's knee and had to run to keep up with his brothers.

"They seem like strong boys and look much like you," the King said to the Mistress. "I cannot say I see much of their fa--"

"Do you doubt I know who their father is? He even claimed them before his people and before God!" the Mistress said.

"I don't doubt you know their father, madam," said the King.

The Mistress quietened, holding her daughter so close the baby began to squall. Her youngest son, intimidated by the raised voices, came to clutch at her skirts. The eldest chose to stand between the King and his mother, small fists clenched. The middle son looked first to his mother before coming to stand behind the eldest.

"The eldest is brave, I will give him that,"

---

[187] Around seven or eight, which means at least one boy had been born before the Countess married their father.

said the King. "And it's time he was in a lord's service. There are many in this procession who, fellow nobles as they are, would be most happy to take on the education of a young earl and baron of the realm."

The Mistress screamed, a quick sudden peal of surprise. Then, "Bow. Bow," she urged the boy. "Bow to your King, child."

"As the Countess has passed without leaving children or, indeed, relatives behind," said the King, "I have no choice but to give her English titles to a suitable candidate who will maintain my law on the Abus."

"Thank you, Sire," the Mistress said with a deep curtsey, finally pushing her eldest son into the bow he was refusing to give.

"I am not entirely sure he is such, but we can raise him to be a noble," said the King.[188]

The eldest son was finally forced into a bow, although his fists stayed clenched.

"I can only give the English estates," the

---

[188] In other words, with the right connections and ties, the boy's loyalties will probably be assured. Along with his mother's.

King said. "And if you should pursue the French title189, I will have your sons all killed for treason."

The Mistress recoiled. "I would never--"

"A woman who claims lands for her children that they have no right to without my gift could also claim lands and titles elsewhere," said the King.

The King called for two nobles in the royal party to come forward. Two men, one elderly and one of his own age, answered the call.

The King pointed to the elder. "This baron has need of a wife's comfort. When he served my father, he won himself a castle and a faithless wife. Fortunately, grandmother is now dead so you, madam, will take up her duties."

"But my children," said the Mistress. "My place here among their father's people..."

"The young children may and will go with you," said the King. "Your eldest, however, will be

---

189 In the real equivalent, the French title (Comte d'Aumale) was taken from Hawise and her third husband in 1196. The English title ("Earl of Aumale or Albemarle) continued with them.

page to your husband's son --" He pointed to the younger man. "-- who will be his guardian. My uncle will ensure that both mine and the new earl's interests are maintained here."

The Mistress opened her mouth and swiftly shut it again without saying anything. She curtseyed.

"My uncle and my grandfather-in-law[190] will continue in the Royal Progress. Your eldest will travel with the party, but you will wait with your other children until your new husband returns for you," said the King.

"As you command, Sire," the Mistress said, and she curtseyed again.

"And I do command it," said the King.

The two noblemen bowed to him.

"As you wish," they said.

"Sire," said the Chaplain, "are we... Are we to have a wedding now?"

---

[190] "Step-", essentially replacing a lost family member like a fairy-tale stepmother replacing the dead mother, and "-in-law", related in the eyes of the law though not by blood, were effectively interchangeable for a long period before settling as they are today.

The King barked with laughter. "Yes, my good Chaplain. Yes, we will indeed."

Chapter Sixteen: In which friends are reunited

The King continued his Royal Progress through the lands that had formerly belonged to the lost Countess but the party were unable to follow the old coast road for too much of it had been lost to the sea. They were forced to turn back to the King's Road in order to find a new route suitable for the whole procession. They passed through the hovel-ridden settlement that marked the remains of the Isle of Ravens without stopping and pushed on to spend the night at the ruined church.

"Sire," the King's young uncle called, "there are peasants camping here.191 Do you wish us to clear them from this place?"

It was the King's grandfather-in-law that answered first. "The Greenwood encroaches on this old church. All manner of luck comes from its people, and it would be best to leave them alone."

His son, the King's uncle, smiled at the response and looked to the King for orders.

---

191 Presumably, they weren't there when the party were travelling in the other direction.

"If there is room for us in the clearing, there is no reason to disturb them all," said the King. "But I would meet with our lowly neighbours, for they may be refugees from the flood and have news of its effects on my land."

"Of course, Sire," his uncle said.

So the uncle entered the church again and returned with five people[192] dressed in yeomen's clothing. Three were clearly men although the third man was supported by the older of the two women, her hands upon his waist and back.

"Sire," said the uncle, "these are the leaders of these peasants."

The King said, "I must admit there are some among you yeomen who look most familiar to me."

The supported man smiled but it was another who answered. "I could say the same of your own party."

"Who do you claim to be, man of Greenwood?" the King's grandfather-in-law asked.

---

[192] I'm not sure why the storyteller does not just say who these five are. It's pretty obvious that these are going to be (in no particular order) John Barleycorn, Dolly, Hugh, the Earl and the Countess.

"I am John Barleycorn," said the one who had spoken193. "These others are my daughter Dolly, our storyteller Hugh, my second Grim194 and his wife Alvive195."

Dolly frowned. "You have the look of someone I once knew, though you are older than I would expect. And you, Sire, could only be a prince of England."

"The King," said Grim. "The true King."

Dolly shrugged.

"I never met nor heard of those last two," said the King's grandfather-in-law.

John Barleycorn smiled. "Should you have?"

"Nor have I, but I recognise them both," said the King.

"Sire," said Grim, sketching a bow around his

---

193 See?
194 The Earl has been renamed for the founder of Grimsby and/or the step-father of Havelock the Dane according to Geoffrey Gaimar and/or Odin. Grim is generally translated from Old Norse to "mask", although the similar and interchangeable Grimnir is usually translated as "hooded one". Just so you know.
195 According to Gaimar, the wife of Grim and mother of Havelock.

wife's hold.

"I'm glad to see you survived the Great Tide," said the King.

He dismounted and approached Grim and his wife, putting his arms around the two of them.

"I had heard that you had been drowned and lost," said the King. "I am happy to find this is untrue, for I would miss such a close, loyal friend."[196]

Alvive said sharply, "And I am happy to find it untrue because I would miss living."

John Barleycorn laughed. "Wouldn't you enjoy the rewards that await you in the next life?"

"I am not ready to find out," she snapped at him.

"You are as charming as you ever were, my dear, and nor am I ready for you to go on and taste your final rewards," the King said.

Alvive glowered but replied, "Thank you, Sire."

"I bring you news of the Isle of Ravens," said the King.

---

[196] Apparently the friendship of a medieval king is free and unconditional.

"It is lost," said Alvive. "We know, Sire." The King nodded.

"As are the Countess and her third husband," said Grim.[197]

"Which is just as well," said Alvive, "as those that survived favoured the Countess's second husband and his mistress over the Countess's true claim."[198]

"I admit, I have granted the Earldom to the scheming Mistress's eldest son," the King said, and he released the two yeomen.

Alvive stepped back but Grim, who she still supported, remained where he was.

"Those in the new village talk as if it were the drowning of old Ys once again," said the King, "as if Countess had been a pagan and her third husband was the devil himself."

"That is a wide-spread tale and it does their campaigning for them," said Hugh.

"I never liked that story," said Grim. "It is another of those created by those who won."[199]

---

[197] The two are specifically disconnecting themselves from the Countess's rights here.

[198] She may be slightly bitter.

"Oh?" asked Hugh.

Grim shrugged. "We only have the word of Gradlon and his priest, or those that side with them, that Dahut was full of sin because she did not survive to tell the story from her view. And such men have a habit of saying it is the women who are full of sin for tempting them with forbidden fruit, not them for choosing to take it."

"I'm not sure it must be one or the other who is full of sin," said Hugh.

"I think that would depend," said Grim, "on whether both knowingly and freely undertake an evil act."

The King's uncle muttered to his father, "I think there is too much discussion of philosophy in this Greenwood of yours."

John Barleycorn snorted.

"You know it isn't true, of course, Sire?" Grim asked the King.

"That Ys was drowned for the Princess's sin? Or that the Countess was not a pagan, nor her husband the devil as red knight?" asked the King

---

199 "History is written by the victors" - Walter Benjamin

with a smile.

Grim did not answer but held his wife, Alvive, closely.

"A king has a duty to protect the souls of his people from corruption and sin, but also earthly threats and damage," said the King. "In this case, it does not matter whether I believe as the Great Tide left behind an estate without a righteous[200] ruler."

"We understand the needs of the kingdom come before those of an earl's family," said Grim, bowing his head. "Besides, the true Countess is lost."

"And she couldn't provide an heir[201], so the title must go elsewhere now she is passed," said Alvive, although there were tears in her eyes.

"You have both served the Countess and myself with good humour[202] and faithful hearts, dear friends," said the King. "I am ashamed that you have become mere yeomen of the Greenwood through my own hand."[203]

---

[200] Rather than "rightful", as the King dispenses all rights.
[201] The implication being that it is the Countess who is or would held at fault in this situation, not her husband.
[202] Not necessarily true.

Dolly said, "There's nothing wrong with Greenwood yeomen, Sire. As your own... grandfather knows well enough."

But the King ignored her, watching Grim and Alvive for their responses.

"We are as happy here as we could have been on the Isle of Ravens," said Alvive, eventually.

Grim said, "And I must go wherever my wife is happy."[204]

"I am happy that you have each other," said the King.

Behind them, John Barleycorn muttered, "And I'm just so happy that everyone's happy."

"It's all we need," said Grim.[205]

---

[203] But not sorry enough to reverse his earlier decision.
[204] Having abandoned the role given to him by the King, his loyalty is to his wife -- who was of higher rank than he when they married.
[205] D'aww!

The Tale of L'île des Corbeaux, as told by Jo M. Thomas

The fairy tale known as L'Île des Corbeaux is generally attributed to Madame d'Aulnoy (1651-1705), the originator of the term, and possibly the genre, of "the fairy tale". However, it cannot be found in the original French collections and is no longer included in English translations. The attribution is disputed due to the language of the one extent French manuscript, which is held in the British Library, being considerably less conversational that Madame d'Aulnoy's usual style and the handwriting could conceivably be another's. The manuscript remains undated.

The first translation of Madame d'Aulnoy's fairy tales into English was in 1699 but the collection was not the complete works as then available in French. However, L'Île des Corbeaux was included under the name The Island of Corby, the translator having gone for a phonetic translation of corbeaux, rather than a literal one. Or possibly just used a regional dialect word for crows.

Originality and Origins

It is debatable whether the tale can be considered "collected" or "written" at this time simply due to the changing definition of an author's role. Originality of a tale was never so important as the way it was told in the period this tale emerged.

Whether collected or written, the tale is generally considered to be the plot of later versions of the <u>Drowning of Ys</u> transposed to an exoticised English location. However, the version of Ys alluded to only crystallised in the late seventeenth century so is of a similar age to our fairy tale. It also didn't receive widespread awareness until the nineteenth century when songs from oral traditions were collected by T. Hersart de la Villemarqué.

<u>L'Île des Corbeaux</u> is also considered to have borrowed heavily from the laies of Marie de France, particularly Bisclavret in making the Earl's character a werewolf of the medieval French tradition. In keeping with Bisclavret, the original French and the early translation both put noticeable effort to ensure that neither the Earl or the Countess are totally evil.

Fixing A Time

It's traditional to assume that fairy tales occur in a some "medieval" period, although many were originally told as if they had only just happened. However, this appears to be intentional with both L'Île des Corbeaux and The Island of Corby. The latter reduces people to their titles (Earl, Countess, King) but the former specifically gives the Countess's title as Comtesse d'Aumale and that the estates in French and English estates were split following her death.

While there have been several Comtesses d'Aumales, there has only been one who held lands in both France and England under that title. Hawise of Aumale held the title from 1179 until 1214. However the French and English titles were split in 1196 when King Philip II of France captured the Norman estate of Aumale. The English title became the Earl of Albemarle and it was used by Hawise's third husband.

A Real Location

The name of English translation leads many

people to assume that Corby in Northamptonshire was intended and then dismiss the story as nonsense. The only other name mentioned in the translation is that of the river, Abus. That said, both versions are dislocated from known English geography and give very little description of the physical location beyond it being an island in the mouth of a river.

This makes location difficult -- until it is remembered that the Abus is an old name for the River Humber and the holdings of the Counts and Earls are looked into. The Aumales/Albemarles were also the Lords of the region known as Holderness in what is now East Yorkshire. This region forms the north bank of the Humber and the coastline there shifts westward at somewhere around two metres per year with a considerable number of known settlements lost since the Domesday Book (1085-1086).

More specifically, there is a spit, now known as Spurn, that comes part way across the mouth of the Humber. This spit has a life-cycle of being rebuilt and destroyed. While there is no destruction that fits within Hawise's window of time, the spit was overrun in the mid-fourteenth century at a time when storm-induced flooding and tidal surges were becoming more common in the North Sea. Indeed, many Danish, German and Dutch settlements were being lost at the same time.

On this occasion of the spit's destruction, there was a settlement known as Ravenserodd or Ravenser Odd on or near the end. The loss (as well as some history) of this drowned port was recorded in the 14th Century <u>Chronicle of Meaux Abbey</u>, which is quite nearby and with family connections. The most relevant description to this explanation reads:

> "The town of Ravenser Odd was an extremely famous borough, devoted to merchandise with many fisheries and the most abundantly provided with ships and burgesses of all the boroughs of that coast. But yet, by all its wicked deeds and especially wrong-doings on the sea, and by its evil actions and predations, it provoked the vengeance of God upon itself beyond measure."

While the traders and ships moved on to Wyke, which became Kingston-upon-Hull, and Grimsby, some of the occupants moved to the mainland end of the spit to Ravenspur or Ravenspurn. It may be that the name Île des Corbeaux is an attempt to translate one or both of these places, where the use of "Raven" relates to a person's name, not directly to a bird.

How this event was captured in a French fairy tale after the connection with France had been lost, however, remains a mystery.

Further Liberties and Additions

This is a retelling in the vein of my earlier attempt with The Knight's Daughter, complete with the inclusion of other tales I felt illustrated parallels well along with differences between this tale and those. However, there is some change in tone due to the differences between the source materials and the subject matter.

My telling follows the plot and tone set by the originals as much as possible and this negates the naive sense of wonder usually associated with retelling less widely known tales. And, having found the Countess and her husband somewhat sympathetic characters, I couldn't resist the urge to give them a happier ending that drowning for their alleged sins.

Still, the gap between the story's path and fact-bound author's sensibilities remain and so the footnotes have once again provided an outlet for both my cynicism and my homework. I apologise for those that became too heavy with historic framework.

The final thing to mention is my removal of magic from the tale in order for the story to work for a modern reader. Medieval works and early fairy tales use magic without considering or mentioning the world behind them, so it is that both Bisclavret and the original version of the Earl both become men in wolf form -- not werewolves as we would think of them thanks to Hollywood -- without there being any question of how they do it nor how it changes their essential nature.

In order to keep the potentially transgressive but otherwise harmless aspects of this magical curse, I have re-imagined the Earl as a transgender man living before hormonal treatment was possible. This means that his assigned sex has to be disguised in order for him to continue to have the rights he has claimed as a man. This is not transgressive because it is a bad thing but because of the need for secrecy and the sense of being outside of what are assumed to be societal norms of the time, just as alluded to in <u>Bisclavret</u> and <u>L'Île des Corbeaux</u>.

Acknowledgements

Once again, my thanks are extended to Sara Smith, who has (again) been a selfless <u>alpha</u> and <u>beta</u> reader. I would also like to thank Hannah Kate Priest for her help with Bisclavret and medieval understandings. I also need to thank my publisher and editor, Michael S. Collins, for allowing me to pursue this research.

I once again owe thanks to Jane Toothill, along with our former colleague Richard Scales, for reading through my descriptions of storms and floodings so that what details I gave held something like reality. Again, any mistakes in that remain mine and not theirs.

My final round of thanks are to Mark and Seonaid Hillyard for being <u>beta</u> readers as well as generally putting up with me -- along with profuse apologies for going for the Welsh phonetic spelling rather than the correct, Scottish Gaelic spelling in the last book. And, as ever, to the Fox Spirit Skulk and my family for their continued support. Fluff will out!

Printed in Great Britain
by Amazon